CHICAGO BOUND 2

Also by the Author...

Chicago Bound

The Reason
(The First Book in the Kate Harrison Detective Series)

Dangerous Souls
(The Second Book in the Kate Harrison Detective Series)

Extradition
(The Third Book in the Kate Harrison Detective Series)

CHICAGO BOUND 2

Time and Again

Dan,

Thank you for
all you do!

Sandra M Colbert

By Sandra M. Colbert

CHICAGO BOUND 2

Windy City Publishers
2118 Plum Grove Road, #349
Rolling Meadows, IL 60008
www.windycitypublishers.com

Published in the United States of America

ISBN:
978-1-941478-87-5

Library of Congress Control Number:
2019914399

WINDY CITY PUBLISHERS
CHICAGO

Dedicated to the joys of lasting friendships~
For Kris, Joan, Cindy, Ruth, and Arlene.

INTRODUCTION

The word "Bound" has several definitions. The one that I relate to the most is from The American Heritage Dictionary—"Inseparably connected with."

I've lived in other cities, in other states in my lifetime, and for reasons that I can never communicate clearly is why I go back so often to the neighborhood of my youth—The Back of the Yards. It was a place that I, for the most part, especially when I became a teenager and beyond, wanted to leave. A place that I was always slightly ashamed of. It was a ruddy place of taverns, two and three flat aged buildings, too many churches, too many languages. I longed for a brick bungalow, preferably a modern light-colored brick near the Marquette Park area. I longed for a neighborhood not defined by its industry and its odor, but of white-collar workers instead of factory workers.

Time and circumstance took me on my lifetime paths, but I kept looking back. I went to antique stores and rifled around looking for ephemera related to Chicago. There was always the old nonfiction book—a couple of them about the Back of the Yards. There were the postcards which usually depicted the stock yards and downtown Chicago.

It was in conversations with people from other places, other cities and states, that I began to realize how unique the neighborhood of my youth was. How steeped in European cultures and history it was. How instrumental it was to the growth of Chicago. But most of all, I realized how much courage and determination it took for these very humble immigrants to make that treacherous journey. A land of opportunity only if you were willing to grind at the most difficult and at times, dangerous jobs for very low wages. A place where you had to work to recreate the elements of the culture and country that you abandoned.

I remain "bound" to that area and to Chicago. I remain bound to the unique memories and to the faded images of the people who left an indelible, and affectionate mark on my soul.

THE PACK OF FOUR

What is it about getting older that makes one so nostalgic? Do we look back because there is so little to look forward to? That view being rather pessimistic, but dreams and plans of our youth no longer apply. We now sail on hoping for the best.

To look back on the so-called good old days has its pitfalls. Memories and time don't always ease the pain of events that we staggered through—they enhance them.

A song, an aroma, a picture can carry one back, despite a mental shield of resistance.

The power of the picture of the four of us on a warm summer day in July, 1963 is always a jolt.

It's a frayed black and white square; four young boys, taken by my sister with her new camera. The four of us before we left for the carnival.

It was called the Free Fair and erupted at the beginning of July for two weeks on the corner of 47th and Damen. Two weeks, when you're a kid, is not long enough for a carnival. It was the highlight of our summer. The place where all the kids hung out even if you didn't have a red cent to spend. The place where we detached from our parents and enjoyed all that was there just for our enjoyment. It was where we spent all the nickels and dimes that we hoarded doing chores and running errands during the rest of the year.

In this picture, I see my thirteen-year-old self, sitting on the front steps of the three-flat where I lived. I'm surrounded by my three best buddies.

Georgie, to my right, with the goofy smile. He loved baseball and played it pretty well. He lived next door in the little bungalow with his Polish immigrant parents. He was an only child. He made us feel like his brothers.

Dan, sitting behind me. Handsome kid. Someone once said he was the quiet one. I never saw that side of him when he was with us. He got teased a lot because the nuns who taught us considered him to be the smartest kid in the class. He did read a lot, even in the summer.

And that's Johnny sitting next to Dan. The three of us smiled at the camera. Johnny stared at the camera. He lived in the weather-worn, wood-frame bungalow across the alley from me. A shabby house with a dead tree in the back that no one ever bothered to cut down.

I had just turned thirteen that month and had caught up with Dan and Georgie. Johnny was a year older than us. Finally, we were all teenagers.

I can't remember when we weren't friends. We called ourselves the Pack of Four. Dan probably thought of that name.

We went to different schools. In this neighborhood, the Back of the Yards, the school that you went to was determined by the country that your parents or grandparents came from.

Mine being Lithuanian, I went to Holy Cross. Dan and Georgie, being of Polish descent, went to Sacred Heart.

Johnny went to Seward School. That was the school that you went to if your parents couldn't afford the Catholic school or if they didn't want to be a part of the religious segregation. The nuns had us pray for the students at Seward School. They were living a life without daily religion, therefore without Jesus. Purgatory would probably be their fate.

Whereas we lived lives full of religion. During the school year, it was mass before class, confession on Saturday and nine o'clock mass on Sunday. We had a lot of reasons to be glad when school was out for the summer.

The day that picture was taken by my sister—who pleaded with us to sit for it since she had a new camera—was a warm, calm summer evening. I was anxious to get going. The rides, the cotton candy, popcorn and the other kids, which now included the girls, were just a few blocks away. Amazing what one's hormone levels can do to a young man's priorities. Suddenly the girls were more than just, well, the girls.

"Can we go now?" Georgie whined.

"We better hurry," Dan said. "This guy's afraid he'll miss the hot dog eating contest."

"No, I ain't," Georgie said. "Just don't want to sit around here all night."

We took off at a rapid clip even though we had been there the past six nights. We knew what was waiting for us and for the most part it was the other kids that we hung out with. That group included the girls. Both Georgie and I had crushes on Marilyn and preened like peacocks around her. Marilyn, of the perfect coiffed black hair and dark eyes, was also the girl who blossomed sooner than the others. We were too young and inexperienced to realize that we were making fools of ourselves.

"Did you hear the new one by the Four Seasons? I got the forty-five today," Georgie yelled at the three of us.

"The whole neighborhood heard it," I said. "It's called *Sherrie* and you played it full blast a hundred times today."

"It's boss," he replied as he jumped up to grab a leaf on a passing tree.

"Man, *Surfin' Safari* is better," Dan said. "Makes me want to live in California. The Beach Boys are cool. So is Jan and Dean."

And on the conversation went until we reached the fair...between three of us.

What one doesn't see when looking at this picture is the bruise on Johnny's face and his arms. We silently ignored the fact, knowing that if we brought it up, it would embarrass and enrage him. We'd seen the bruises before. We knew his father was a drunk: a mean drunk, a subject of neighborhood gossip that even us kids couldn't ignore.

Johnny was smart, with a quick wit that he often used on us. There was always a remark or a joke, usually dirty, that had us in fits of laughter. But then there was the cruel, cutting remark made to one of us that ended up with something of an apology when he saw the reaction.

"I'm only kidding, man. Don't be such a baby."

The offended one would shrug it off. "No big deal."

Johnny was our leader. We secretly idolized him. He had the self-assurance and confidence that we lacked. He had the swagger.

He was my best friend.

That night he was quiet. He hardly uttered a word in the hour since we'd met up.

When we got to the fair, we separated. Dan and Georgie took off towards the Ferris wheel where they would join the rest of the kids that we hung around with. Johnny nudged me in the other direction.

"I'm starving. Let's get a dog," he said.

"Yeah, me too," I said. I had eaten dinner, but there was something so good about a hot dog at the carnival.

He still hadn't said much. I sensed that he still didn't want to talk, and I allowed that for him. This wasn't the first time.

I was surprised, though, when he ordered two dogs, two bags of chips, and two Pepsis.

He looked over at me, smiled and said, “My treat.”

It was when he drew out a wad of cash from the pocket of his jeans that I knew I had to say something.

I waited until we were at the picnic table and began to dig into the food that I asked,

“John, where the heck did you get all that cash?”

“My old man,” he replied, with an air of casualness.

“Your old man. Your old man gave you that cash?”

“He didn’t give it to me. I took it when he passed out.”

“You took it. Are you nuts? He’s gonna kill you!”

There was no hiding my shock… and fear.

“Yeah, like he hasn’t tried that already.”

I didn’t know how to respond to that, so I didn’t. He slipped back to silence. The conversation wasn’t over.

My stomach turned. I dropped the hot dog on the table and swigged my Pepsi.

When he finished his dog, he nodded to me and said, “Let’s go.”

“Maybe you can put it back before he misses it,” I said, sounding as anxious as I felt.

“Ain’t doing that.”

“But John—”

“I ain’t doing that because I ain’t going back there.”

“You ain’t going back where?”

The din of the carnival was getting on my nerves. I suddenly wanted to be away from this place.

He didn’t answer me but headed towards the 47th street entrance. I followed. We plowed by the people walking into the carnival.

“It’s like this, lame brain,” he said when I caught up to him. “I ain’t going back to that house with the drunk shit of a father and useless mother. I ain’t going back.”

I grabbed his arm and made him turn and face me. I could hear a voice announcing the start of the pie eating contest.

“What are you talking about? Where you gonna go?” It came out as a whine. “I don’t get it, man.”

“What’s not to get. You see all these bruises. The son of a bitch coulda killed me last night. Ya wanna know why?”

I was afraid to hear why. All I could manage was a feeble shrug.

"Cuz he was beating up my old lady and I got in the middle of it. I called him every name I could think of, but he's bigger and stronger and just beat me up. So I ain't going back."

My mind flashed to my parents. My gentle father, an accountant at the neighborhood bank, never even spanked me. My stay-at-home mother, who seemed to always be baking our favorite cookies, was the disciplinarian who doled out the punishments, which usually meant bed without dinner or more chores. Neither parent spent much time in any of the taverns which dotted each block. If they did go, it was with friends and they never came home drunk.

"John, whadya gonna do? Ya got go somewhere."

He took me by the elbow and led me across the street to the bus stop.

"I'm takin' the next bus to Ashland. From Ashland I'm taking a bus to downtown and getting on a Greyhound bus."

"What? That doesn't make sense. Then go where?"

He didn't answer.

"John, John, you can't do that. You're just a kid."

"I ain't a kid."

Panic surged through me. This couldn't be happening. Kids didn't get beaten. Kids didn't get on buses and take off.

"You are. You're still a kid," I repeated.

He shoved me against a lamppost.

"You say that again and you'll have some bruises," he said. "I'm fourteen and I ain't a kid. I don't know if I was ever a kid, like you and Dan and Georgie. I've been taking care of myself for a real long time. My old lady too lazy or drunk half the time to even make me something to eat. My old man just too drunk. I wash my clothes and make the food. She does it sometimes, but it's mostly me taking care of me."

I never knew any of this. I should have. He was my best friend. My throat tightened and I fought back tears.

"Come to my house," I said. I knew it was not the solution, but my best friend couldn't just go away.

"Yeah, right. Your folks are gonna let me live with them. And what happens when my mother and old man find out? They'll drag me out of there and beat the shit out of me."

"Don't you have grandparents?" Another fact that I should have known.

"Hers live in Texas. I never even met them. His, I don't know. He never talks about them. I think I met them once when I was little. Don't know nothing about them."

I looked down the street and prayed that the bus wouldn't come.

"We gotta think of something, John. You can't just take off. Where you gonna go?" I said, not disguising the panic that I was feeling.

"My brother took off a long time ago. He lives in Michigan. I'll go to him. I don't think he'll tell the old man. He'll be cool. I ain't seen him since I was little."

"You got his address?"

"Yeah, it's old but I think he's still there."

"For how long? You gotta come back to go to school."

"You don't get it, do you? I ain't coming back."

"John, you have to."

"No, I don't."

"You're my best friend, John."

"And you're my best friend. The best any guy could have. But, I gotta go. I can't live like this no more."

He gave me a sliver of a smile.

"Here's the thing," he continued. "You can't tell no one. You gotta promise me this, Pete. You can't tell Dan or Georgie or no one. If the old man finds me, I'm as good as dead."

When I didn't respond, he grabbed me by my shoulders.

His face inches from mine, he said, "You gotta promise. You don't tell no one about the bus or about Michigan or nothing that I just told you."

I nodded.

"Say you promise. As my best friend you gotta promise."

"I promise, John. I promise."

"Good. You're a good guy. You'll keep your promise."

He looked down the street. The bus was in the distance. Once again, I was swallowing back tears.

"I don't want you to go."

"Thing is, I don't want to go. But what else can I do. He'll kill me some day or I'll kill him. I gotta go."

The bus was getting closer.

"Write to me, John. Tell me where you're at. I won't tell no one."

"Yeah, sure. I'll send you a letter once in a while."

The bus made its metal-on-metal sound when it stopped feet from us. Out poured the latest carnival-goers—the giggling kids and the grinning adults.

"John,"

"Yeah?"

I hugged him. There were no words for what I was feeling.

He hugged me back, kept his head down and got on the bus. He didn't look back. I wanted him to. I watched as the doors of the bus closed. I watched as it drove away. I watched the back of that green bus until I could no longer see it. Only then did I go back to the carnival.

I staggered past the cotton candy stand and stuffed animal booths, past the people throwing ping pong balls into colored goldfish bowls. I stopped when I heard Dan calling me.

"Hey man, where you been? Where's Johnny?"

"He went home." My first lie. "Said he wasn't feeling so hot."

Dan nodded.

"He wasn't looking so hot. That lousy son-of-a-bitch father of his."

"Yeah. I think I'm gonna go home too."

"What? Why? We just got here."

"I don't know. I'm just kinda bored. We been here almost every night."

"Marilyn was asking about you. You can't go," he said. "What happened? You and Johnny have a fight."

"No," I snapped. "Jesus, I just want to go home. Is that alright with you?"

"Okay, okay, just go. I'll tell Marilyn that Georgie is all hers."

I started to walk away.

"Pete," he called to me. "You all right?"

"Yeah, I'm fine. See ya tomorrow."

"Sure, yeah. See ya tomorrow."

I ran all the way home. With a sense of relief I remembered that my parents and sister wouldn't be there that evening. My hands shook when I tried to put the key in the lock. I stomped through the empty flat screaming every curse word I had ever heard at Johnny's parents. I cursed at myself for being the incapable friend who should have helped him and didn't. When I was spent, I collapsed on my bed and wept harder than I ever had in my life.

The next day was filled with the news that Johnny hadn't come home that night. By that afternoon, his mother finally went to the police station and told them that he hadn't come home the night before and no one knew where he was.

I could barely hide my hatred when the two of them showed up at our back door, both reasonably sober, to ask me if I knew where Johnny was. I almost enjoyed that lie.

It was harder to lie to Dan and Georgie and then to repeat the lie to the police when they showed up a day later.

"No," I told all of them. "I don't know where he is. Just said he wanted to go home. He was bored and didn't have any money to spend, so why hang around." I liked my embellishment about the money.

Suddenly, it was a Pack of Three. Georgie kept saying that Johnny would show up. He was probably on some kind of an adventure, he said. He started fabricating stories about these adventures until we told him to shut up.

Then he would look down the street as if Johnny would suddenly appear.

Dan remained silent. So did I.

It was hard to watch the hope turn to grief. By the time September came along and another school year started Johnny was rarely mentioned. When he was, one of us usually ended up wiping away a tear.

Life went on. Mine with a gaping hole in it. He never did write. I didn't think he would. I just prayed that he was alright. I prayed that he was living in some small town in Michigan with his brother and new friends.

Time careened by. High school overtook us. For a while we still saw a lot of each other, but something always felt off, like a table with three legs. It wasn't long before we went down separate paths with different friends. The specter of Johnny seemed to hang over us.

After high school, Dan went on to college on a full scholarship. He was on his way to a Ph.D.

I joined the National Guard.

Georgie was drafted. Vietnam now a part of the daily rhetoric.

Georgie didn't return. His mother's wailing scarred my soul.

The day of the service, Dan and I met at the funeral parlor. It had been a while since we had seen each other. We gave each other a hug but were equally unable to speak. Dan placed Georgie's baseball mitt on top of the coffin as it was lowered.

It was after the funeral luncheon at the bar on the corner and after we had a few drinks that we walked to the now shuttered grocery store across from the houses where Georgie and I once lived. We brought bottles of Schlitz from the bar and took our swigs. We laughed at nothing. It kept us from weeping.

"You know what happened to Johnny," Dan stated. I wasn't surprised. It had to come up.

Instead of answering, I walked into the gangway and vomited.

"You were weird that night. I know something happened between the two of you. It was written all over your face."

I wiped my mouth and looked over at him. I remained silent. I didn't want to lie any more.

"You'll never tell."

I wanted to. I couldn't form the words.

"You're an honorable man," he said.

"Like hell I am. I am not an honorable man. Now Georgie, our dear friend, our best buddy, now there was an honorable man. Me? Maybe I'm just real good at keeping secrets."

"Even if it means being a real prick."

"Yep. Don't hate me for it."

"I don't hate you, bud. I'll never hate you. You're a part of my memory bank, a good part."

He stood up and looked around.

"It's all changing, Pete. Everything is fucking changing. Look at this neighborhood. I don't know anyone who lives here anymore. I don't live here anymore. You don't live here anymore, and God know Georgie doesn't live here anymore. He don't live nowhere."

He probably didn't realize that he was yelling.

"And this little grocery store has been closed for two years now."

"And your point is?" I asked.

"My point. My point, buddy is that I want to go back. I want Johnny and Georgie and you and me. I want to go to Sox games and to the show and most of all I want to go to that damn Free Fair carnival thing."

"Me too, Dan. Me too."

He pointed his now-empty beer bottle at me.

"Stay in touch, you secret keeping son of a bitch. Stay in touch."

He staggered away, belting out the Four Seasons song, *Sherrie.*

Dan did go on to get his Ph.D. and became a professor of history at a nearby university. He wrote a few books about Chicago that were well received. Over the years I would see him on documentaries about Chicago. But I didn't stay in touch. Neither did he. I saw him several times over the years, twice at his book signings. But we had little to say to each other.

That secret hung over us.

Me? I played it safe, as I was prone to do. After the National Guard, I went to a community college and ended up in banking like my dad. Got married, moved to the suburbs, had two kids, now have grandkids.

It's those warm summer nights—nights when I choose to be alone with my thoughts—that Johnny is resurrected. I wrap myself in the memories of the Pack of Four; Johnny, Dan, Georgie and me. I see the old neighborhood, the carnival and the faces of those long gone.

I bring out the old photograph, wipe away a tear or two then smile at the blessings of friendship and youth.

THE BREADMAKER

Gramma had her ritual. It was always on a Saturday morning. Bring out the bowl and pans—the same thick, glazed bowl and the darkened, dented pans used for decades of making bread. The bags of flour, salt, and sugar were set out in front of her. A pitcher of water and the readied yeast off to the side.

Turn on the Lithuanian radio station.

After reviewing the items on the table and with a blow of her breath, she began.

I watched her go through her ritual dozens of times as a child. I often asked her if I could do something. I wanted to create this magic. I was too young, she would say. Not strong enough. Not tall enough. Looking back, I believe that this ritual was something that she simply didn't want to relinquish to anyone. This was hers, solely hers. She was considered the best bread maker in the neighborhood. She not only made bread for us, but for others on the block. When there was a death in a family, when there was a birth in a family, Gramma brought bread. When there was a special occasion of any kind, Gramma brought bread.

I would sit on a chair near the table, not too close, of course, and watch the ingredients come together under her hands. To me it was magical. Of course, there was no recipe. She deftly threw together the ingredients in the bowl and before long, it was on the floured table. Under her hands, it was transformed into dough. I watched as she pushed her hands into the dough, then pulled it, then pushed it, repeatedly. The kneading; this was my favorite part. The dough morphing into something that would soon be warm, succulent bread.

"Raisins today, Gramma?" I would ask. I knew not to assume that there would be raisins.

"No, no raisins today," she would say. Sensing my disappointment, she assured me that I would have the first warm slice, with as much butter as I wanted.

That put a smile on my face. There was usually a battle with my brother and little sister when the bread came out of the oven. We waited around the kitchen, soaking in the warmth of the room bathed with the aroma of the bread. It was Gramma who removed the loaves from the pans. It was Gramma who cut the first slice and determined who got it. It was a game we played. If we did something in the course of the week that pleased her, an extra chore or a good report card, we got the first slice.

The question about the raisins was the only one I was allowed to ask. Gramma never spoke when making bread. Gramma was not a chatty person. She did her share of gossiping with her lady friends, but she was the one quiet one, the least animated, the least outraged.

I broke this rule one day. At twelve I was becoming curious about so many things. And keeping quiet, at times, was difficult for me.

"Gramma, did your mother make bread like you?" I asked.

She froze, her hands imbedded in the dough. The kneading stopped for what seemed to me a very long time.

"Gram?"

She snapped out of her reverie. She turned to look at me. I saw it in her eyes. I wanted to take back the question. I wanted to leave the room.

It was pain I saw. Not a sweet memory I thought she would want to share, but raw pain.

"Yes, yes," she said in a voice so low, it was almost inaudible.

With a shake of her head, she went back to the kneading, only at a much slower pace. She put the mass of dough in the large ceramic bowl and covered it with a dish towel. It was time for the bread to rise. Only then did she look back at me.

"She make best bread in village. Always the best."

"Like you?"

She smiled.

"Like me."

I knew the conversation would go no further. I helped her with the clean-up. There were chores to do and errands to run.

The radio was turned off and the paced quickened. She handed me two dollar bills with instructions on what to get from the grocery store across the street. I left.

When I returned with the bag of groceries, Gramma was sitting in her bedroom staring at a picture. She held it out for me to see. It was a tattered, small black-and-white photo the size of a post card. The image—a group of people, the women in black dresses and babushkas, the men in ill-fitting dark suits. They stood behind a wooden coffin—a coffin that held a woman dressed in peasant clothes, her arms crossed over her chest.

I looked over at Gramma. She was wiping away tears.

"Your mother?" I said softly.

"Mama, my mama. She make best bread."

I had never seen this picture before. Slowly, reluctantly, I handed it back to her. I kissed her cheek.

I walked out of the flat. I left her to clutch her memories.

THE SIN

The click-clacking of the streetcar felt like small daggers being driven into her head. And the shaking of her hands—she didn't know if it came from the jostle of the streetcar or from her already frazzled nerves.

When Mary looked out through the soot-tinged windows, all she could see was gray—steely, bleak gray. The sky, the buildings, the very air itself looked gray, varying shades of gray. It seemed like the sun didn't come to this part of town.

But the stench did, being even closer to the stockyards. The smell did nothing to quell the nausea the she was feeling.

She looked over at her older sister.

"How much farther?" she asked.

"Coupla stops." Jen replied.

"It's worse here. I thought our neighborhood was the shits."

"Not a great part of town, that's for damn sure."

She turned back to the window. It was the children that she noticed now. Different ages, some boys, some girls, all with the rag-like clothes, with dirt encrusted on them like a second skin.

She tried to shake off the nausea.

"You gonna be sick?" Jen asked, seeing her sister's discomfort. "We'll be getting off soon."

Mary gulped, then took a deep breath.

"I'll be all right."

Once off the streetcar, Mary stopped walking. She looked around at the brick streets and the wooden sidewalks.

"At least we have paved streets and real sidewalks, not this rotten wood shit," Jen said.

"Yeah, we got it made—a real ritzy neighborhood."

"Come on, this way," Jen said, leading her sister toward a nearby alley.

"Fer Christ sake, Jen, we have to go through the alley? Isn't the street bad enough?"

"We don't want nobody to see where we're going so yeah, we go in through the alley."

Mary kept her head down and followed her sister.

"Jen."

"What?"

"How'd you find out about this place?"

Jen stopped walking, took out a cigarette and lit it before answering.

"Women talk. They ask around. Then they find out stuff. Everybody knows somebody."

"But why were you asking?"

"Why the hell do you think? I got knocked up after a couple of dates with Johnny. I didn't want any damn kid messing things up. I didn't want Johnny to marry me cuz I was knocked up. And I wasn't about to listen to Ma and everybody telling me what a tramp I was. I'd never hear the goddamned end of it. And I was having fun. Me and Johnny were getting along just great. This would ruin everything. He would end up marrying me cuz I had a kid coming, not because he wanted to. Turns out he wanted to anyway. But at least we had a coupla good years before the kids showed up."

Mary stared in silence at her sister, then lit her own cigarette.

"Why didn't you tell me, Jen? Geez," she said.

"You were just a kid. You didn't need to know. Nobody needed to know."

"Did you come here alone?"

"No. Some old lady brought me. I met her on 47th and Ashland, on the corner, we got on that same streetcar. I had to give her a couple of bucks. Like I said, women talk. I'm not telling you no more. You don't need to know any more of this shit," she said. "Let's go before a rat starts nibbling at our heels."

Mary followed her sister down an unpaved, mud-encrusted alley, bypassing the rusted, overflowing garbage cans.

They turned into a gangway—a blackened tunnel made black by the two three-story buildings on either side. It was a rancid walkway where the sun refused to shine. They fumbled their way to a door in the middle of the building on the right. Yellowed dim bulbs lit their way up a staircase to the top floor. The smell of cooking cabbage assaulted them.

When Jen opened the door, a bell tinkled, not unlike the bell at the grocery store on their block.

The room was a kitchen with chairs instead of kitchen furniture. No stove or refrigerator or table. All the chairs were occupied.

Three women and a girl were in this small room.

A buxom woman, staring at the floor, her eyes filled with resignation and sadness.

Another, a tall, buxom woman, nicely dressed. A cigarette balanced in her lips, she looked proud, proud and angry. Shoulders back, defiant.

The third, a young girl sitting crookedly on her chair, chewing her thumb, unbridled fear on her face. Mary thought that she could not have been older than fifteen and prayed that she was wrong. An older woman sat in rigid silence next to the girl. Mary assumed it was her mother, but after what Jen had told her, it could have been anyone.

From another room, a bedroom, a man sauntered out—short, bespectacled, with wisps of gray hair on top of his balding head. He wore a blood-stained butcher's apron. His hands held a bloody instrument.

He bellowed to the women in the room.

"Fer Cris sake. Not another one. Can't you god-damned dames stop spreading your legs? If you did, you wouldn't be in this mess."

Mary felt her entire body tremble. She gripped Jen's arm to keep from falling.

"Is it both of you?" the butcher continued.

"No," Jen spoke up. "Just her."

"You got the money? It's fifty bucks."

"Don't worry about it. We got it," Jen answered, displaying a toughness Mary wished she had.

"I got three ahead of you. You can wait or come back another time."

"We'll wait."

"Fine." With a shake of his head he walked back into the room he came from.

A moan cut through the air shortly after he went back in.

Another wave of nausea hit Mary. She prayed she could keep it down, but the smells of the place and the fear that was engulfing her made things worse. She wished for a place to sit.

A short time later, an older woman walked out of the room. She wore a babushka and a butcher's apron as well. She carried a bucket and walked toward the outside door, past Mary and Jen.

Mary looked down at the bucket as the woman walked past.

The bucket sloshed with a watery red liquid and with what could have been a liver from the butcher shop that Mary sometimes went to.

She ran from the room, pushing the old lady aside.

When Jen caught up with her, Mary was vomiting next to a garbage can. A nearby rat watched.

Jen found a rock and hurled it at the rat and waited for her sister's heaves to stop.

When they did, she handed her a handkerchief.

Mary broke down in sobs.

"I can't do it, Jen," she said, hysterics forming in her voice. "I just can't. The man is a butcher. I can't. I can't. I can't do it. He'll kill me. Did you see him, all covered in blood? Did you see that? And the smell."

"Calm down, Mary," Jen said. She gripped her trembling sister by the shoulders. "If you don't want to do this, maybe we can figure something else out. I don't know what, but we will."

She added, "But I ain't coming back here again. Make up your mind. We go back in there and get it done or we go home."

Wiping her tears, Mary looked back at the foul, squalid building that she just run from. Until now she had pushed aside the thoughts of that awful night, of the filthy hands pushing her against a wall in the alley—the foul breath, the threats, the grunts, the pain.

In her mind he was a monster—something out of a horror movie. Large and filthy. The typical walk home from work on a dark February evening turned into an unspeakable nightmare. She now walked blocks out of her way. At times she walked down the middle of the street. But the fear remained, unabated, constant.

It was Jen who found her in the bathtub of their parent's small flat. Stopping in for a short visit with her mother, Jen found the flat empty aside from Mary, who said she was taking a bath. Impatient and getting concerned with the amount of time Mary was spending in the bathroom, Jen burst in, no longer interested in her sister's excuses.

One look at her younger sister, with the bruises forming on her thin body, that Jen, to her horror, understood what had happened. It was the look on Mary's face, the look Jen knew she would never forget—the streaming tears, the quiver of her lips, the anguish in her young eyes.

"Do I have a choice, Jen? What else can I do? I can't have a monster's baby. It might not even be a human."

Jen said a silent prayer.

God help her. How damaged was her sister? She's so young. Can she ever get over this? If we go back in. will she ever get over what will happen there? Please, God help her and forgive her.

"Let's go back," Mary said, gripping her sister's hand. "Maybe, if I'm lucky, the butcher will finish me off."

"Don't talk like that. Hell, I survived. I'm fine."

"That's just it, Jen. I'm not fine. Don't know that I'll ever be. I feel like I'm breaking apart, ya know, in my head. The dreams, they don't quit. I see those yellow eyes. He had yellow eyes. I told you that Jen, didn't I?"

"Yeah, you told me."

"I have a couple of shots every night now before I go to bed."

"Yeah, I know that too. Be careful, ma or pa might start noticing."

"It helps, Jen, a little at night. I try to stay busy during the day, but I still get the shakes. I'm scared all the time."

"I know, Mary. I know. But it'll pass. Someday this will be some shitty memory and you'll be fine. You'll see."

"God, Jen, I hope you're right. Cuz I just don't feel right in my head no more. And I'm dirty now. Inside, ya know? I can't never get married. What do I tell some guy? Do I tell him about this or about the monster? No, can't never get married."

"Don't talk like that. You're not the first that this happened to and, it's a goddamn shame, but you ain't gonna be the last," Jen said.

She took her trembling sister in her arms.

"Mare, we have to do this thing," Jen said. "You have to do this thing."

"I know, Jen. I know," Mary looked back at the building. "So let's go back to that shithole and the butcher. We gotta kill the monster's baby. Then maybe I'll be better."

"Yeah, little sister. You'll be better. You'll see. You'll be better. "

PRESCOTT, ARIZONA

"Terrie," her co-worker said, somewhat timidly, "There's a customer out here who wants to open up a checking account."

"Really, Karen? I'm at lunch." Terrie replied, making no attempt to hide her annoyance.

"I know, but we are so shorthanded today, there's no one else out there who can help him."

"What happened to Jonathan?"

"I had to put him on the teller line to relieve for lunch."

"Great. So I get to skip mine."

Karen didn't respond.

"Fine," she snapped. "I'll be right out."

She took a bite of her sandwich and shoved the rest in the refrigerator with her bottle of water.

Damn this job, she muttered to the empty kitchen. One year and one month to retirement. I hope I make it without beating someone senseless.

She walked out scowling and knew she had to force a smile for the customer—the customer that someone had already brought to her desk.

With only a slight glance in his direction, she logged on to her computer, mechanically said her name, and asked how he was.

He was thin, in need of a shave. His disheveled gray hair looked like it was ready for a cut. The faded Grateful Dead tee-shirt and worn jeans completed the old hippie/mountain man look.

He probably only has twenty bucks to his name and will want a car loan with his checking account.

She asked for his driver's license while pulling up the new account screen.

She began to ask him another question but froze, mid-sentence, when she saw the name on the license.

Slowly, deliberately, she looked up from the document in her hand to the man sitting across the desk from her.

It can't be. It's impossible.

But it was. Those intense, deep brown eyes. Those lips.

"Frank?" she said, almost in a whisper.

The recognition hit him with the same jolt.

"Terrie?"

CHICAGO—1970

Terrie had heard about this place from her friends, especially those who followed the music scene in Chicago, but this was the first time that she had been to the Aragon Ballroom.

She tried to imagine what it was like in the day—the 1930s, '40s and '50s. She looked around at the mosaic tiles, the beautiful arches that surrounded the dance floor, the terra cotta ceiling, now covered with years of grime, a shabby reflection of what this place had once been. The big band's brass sections now gave way to huge black amplifiers. The audience, once well-dressed teens slow dancing or jitterbugging, replaced with hippies and the smell of pot.

Her aunt had once told her that she had went there often with her then fiancé, now her husband. They would dance far into the night to the music of the big swing bands that came through Chicago —Count Bassie, Glenn Miller, Artie Shaw.

That hadn't changed. The big groups still played the Aragon. Tonight, it was Steve Winwood and Traffic, one of her favorites. Terrie and her three girlfriends wormed their way through the crowd to get a place near the stage where they were meeting Clare's boyfriend Danny and his friends.

Her three friends; Clare, Jane, and Nancy met in high school and continued their friendship into college. The University of Illinois at Circle Campus, as it was then called, being the only affordable one for the four girls from the southwest side of the city. Terrie, Jane, and Nancy were not seeing anyone and hoped that there may be more to this concert than music.

The music scene of the '60s was vibrant and exciting, reflecting not only the turbulent times but the huge array of talent coming from all directions. The girls and their friends, both male and female, filled their free time at the many music venues the city had to offer. If they weren't seeing a group perform, the topics, when they got together, were about the latest albums and who was breaking into the music scene.

Clare spotted Danny in the crowd. He had gotten there before them and saved a space on the floor. The Aragon, being a former dance venue, did not have seats. You simply sat on the floor. He had his friends with him, two of whom the girls knew from the neighborhood. Terrie noticed the one newcomer.

Danny introduced him. "Ladies, here is the newest addition to our little group. He goes by the name of Frank. We have other names for him, but you can call him Frank." Frank, in response, gave an unsmiling nod to the girls and turned away, appearing more interested in the equipment on the stage than any of them. His dark hair was long, but not as long as many of the guys in this crowd. His clothes typical—a khaki green army jacket, tee shirt and worn jeans.

His dark eyes stayed on the stage. He swayed back and forth to music that had not yet started.

"What's the story with him?" Terrie asked Claire as soon as they were settled and had a chance to talk.

"Frank?" she responded. "I just met him for the first time last weekend. He got back from Vietnam a few weeks ago. Danny and the guys grew up with him. They're kinda trying to help him get back to normal, you know, after all that he's seen. He's real quiet. I didn't talk to him much."

"He on drugs?" Jane asked. "He seems weird."

"Could be. He's probably seen a lot of shit. This has to be tough on him," Claire said. "Danny said he's a really good guitar player. He wants to get a band together."

"He's really cute," Terrie added. "Kinda looks like Jackson Browne."

"Yeah, kinda," Claire said. "But he's taken. Has a girlfriend from high school that he got back together with when he got home."

"Wonder why she's not here with him," Terrie said, staring intently at the man.

"Hmm." Jane responded. "I don't think I like that look in your eyes, Ter. He's taken and he's probably kind of messed up. A lot of these guys coming back are. A lot of them are hooked on drugs that they got from the Vietnamese. Steer clear. There are other fish in the sea."

Terrie nodded and turned her attention to the stage, where the performers were gathering. Despite Jane's comments, Terrie couldn't stop herself from glancing over toward Frank throughout the concert. She saw something—an intensity, a gentleness that came through his dark eyes.

He's different, she thought. *He's not like the other guys here. But he's taken. Shake it off.*

But she couldn't shake it off. By the end of the show, she had spent more time watching Frank then Steve Winwood.

After the show, they all agreed to meet at the small neighborhood restaurant owned by Danny's father, where they had the run of the place. Tonight, Danny and eight of his friends converged. His father frowned when he saw them.

"As long as they all order something and you don't be giving them free food, I'm alright with all of them coming here. I'll stay open longer tonight, but when I say we're closed, we're closed."

"Okay, Dad. Don't sweat it," Danny replied.

The little group took up three booths. Frank sat across from Terrie. He was more animated and friendlier than at the concert. Terrie struck up a conversation about the show and what groups she had seen recently. He wanted to catch up on the music scene, he told her. He missed so much of what was happening, because of Vietnam.

The more he spoke and the more he made eye contact, the more smitten Terrie became.

By the end of the night, she was convinced that he was as attracted to her as she was to him.

"You two seemed to hit it off," Nancy said in the car on their way home.

"Uh, yeah," Jane piped in. "Don't get carried away, Ter. He is really taken."

"No, he can't be. He just can't be," Terrie responded. "I like him. I mean I really like him. And I think he likes me."

"Uh, oh," Jane said. "Don't like the sound of that."

"Did you see those eyes? God, he's gorgeous."

"Terrie, he was smoking pot all evening. Those were stoned eyes. God knows what he was doing with those guys in the car on the way here. He may not even remember you tomorrow, especially when he's with his girlfriend."

"Yeah, just a girlfriend. It's not like he's married."

"I'm too tired to talk about it. And I got a headache. Think I sat too close to the amps. Call me tomorrow," Jane said.

"I will," Terrie said as she was dropped off at her house.

"Call me too," Nancy added. "I think you're going to need to talk more about this Frank thing."

Terrie knew sleep wouldn't come. She replayed the conversations. She thought back to his features, the eyes, the dark hair. How did someone so soft-spoken and gentle ever serve in Vietnam? It didn't seem possible that he could be a hard-nosed grunt capable of killing people.

She looked out the window at the dawn of the new day, more determined than ever to win him over.

He's not engaged. He's not married. He was attracted to me. I could feel it. I know it. We belong together.

With her friends' support, even over their objections, Terrie set about getting together with Frank. Most of the time it was at Danny's restaurant, other times at concerts.

The girlfriend did show up on several occasions. Terrie and company all found fault with her on different levels. They all decided not to use her name.

"Persona non grata," Nancy said. "No chatting with her, girls. We may end up liking her."

"What does she have that I don't?" Terrie asked.

"Nothing. I don't get the attraction," Jane responded, now in full support of her friend. "You're cuter, smarter. Maybe it's just loyalty."

When they found out that he was taking classes at Circle, as the University was referred to, they devised a system of communicating to Terrie where he was spotted and when his classes let out.

At these encounters with Terrie, he was always friendly and talkative. But he never crossed an invisible line, to Terrie's frustration and pain.

"I'm in love with him," she admitted to the girls over drinks one evening. "Now I know the true meaning of unrequited love. Here I thought it was something in romance novels. But it's real."

"Terrie, nothing is happening. Face it," Nancy said. "You have to get over him. If something was going to happen, it would have happened by now. Time to get real. This has been going on for months now. And to be honest, I think he's starting to look a little uncomfortable around you."

"Nancy's right," Jane said. "I think if anything was going on, he would have said something to Danny. He's pretty close to Danny and I think if your name came up, Dan would say something to me. And all this spying is wearing me out."

"You're probably right. No, I *know* you're right, but how do I do that? He's in my head all the time. I can't just shake him off."

"First of all, stop going where he goes and stop accidently, on purpose, bumping into him on campus," Jane said. "If it's meant to happen, it'll happen."

"And he's still seeing what's-her-face," Claire added. "It seems that they're together more than ever."

"Time to move on, Terrie," Jane said. "Time to get over him. It's just not happening."

Terrie wiped away a tear and looked away.

"Glad I'm not driving. Time to get drunk," she said to her friends.

A few months into the second quarter, Terrie quit going to school and took a job at a downtown bank, citing financial reasons to her friends. This was true but only partially. They all knew a small part of her decision had to do with her not wanting to run into Frank anymore, especially when he was with his girlfriend. Her friends never doubted her when she said that she was in love with him. Once when Terrie wasn't around, they made a pact not to mention his name. They would do what they had to do to help her get over this futile one-sided affair.

Almost a year after starting the job at the bank, Terrie took a call at work from Claire.

"I have to tell you something," Claire said. "Brace yourself."

"What?"

"Frank's engaged to what's-her-face."

Terrie froze. She couldn't respond.

"Danny just called and told me. All the guys are excited for him."

Terrie remained silent.

"Ter, you still there?"

"Yes, I'm still here."

"You okay?"

"Yeah, fine. Not a big deal, right? Not like we dated or anything. Haven't seen him in ages."

"You don't sound fine."

"I'm not," she conceded. "I've got to go. Thanks for letting me know."

Terrie shuffled papers on her desk with shaking hands before telling her supervisor she was going on break. She found an empty bathroom stall, where she beat the wall before she silently wept.

PRESCOTT, ARIZONA

"Oh my God, Frank, I can't believe it's you. It can't be. How is this even possible?" she said, her voice quivering, her heartbeat racing.

"I can't believe it either. Damn, Terrie, it's been what? How many years?" he answered with a broad smile.

"Forget years. Decades. This is incredible. What are you doing in Prescott?"

Please, she thought. *I pray that I don't look as rattled as I feel.*

"I could ask you the same thing."

"You first."

"Teaching music, when I'm not a substitute teacher at the high school. Moved here about six months ago. I figured it was about time that I opened an account here. And you?"

She took a deep breath, hoping to calm down enough to answer.

"Been in Arizona about fifteen years. Lived in Phoenix for five of them before coming up here."

"With your family?"

"Uh, no, divorced. One of the reasons I left Chicago. New start, you know."

"Yeah, I know. Shelly and I, you remember Shelly, don't you?"

"Yes, Yes, I do." *Persona non grata. The nameless one.*

"We got married. Lasted for about fifteen years. Just couldn't make it work. She found someone else and I've been wandering around ever since. Lived in Michigan, then Montana for awhile. Hated the winters, then about ten years in San Diego before moving here. It became too expensive and crowded for me. I checked this place out and here I am. A much better fit."

"Teaching music the whole time?"

"Yeah, I make some money doing private lessons too. I like being around kids and music. Keeps me young."

"No kids of your own?"

"No. Shelly couldn't get pregnant, which in retrospect might have been a good thing. I was a lousy husband. Too moody and selfish. But it would have been nice to have a kid. It might have made me a better person. I think a lot of how different things would have been if we had a kid. Anyway, we're on good terms. She remarried and I get to roam around the country and do what I want."

Terrie didn't respond. To her, it was a life that rang of loneliness.

"And you? Any kids?"

"A daughter, Chelsea. Um, strangely enough, she's a teacher at the grammar school down the street."

"Really? What does she teach? What grade?

Facing away from him, she mumbled, "Second grade and music."

He looked down at his hands, a sudden awkward silence between them.

"It's been a lot of years, Terrie."

"It has. It really has."

"You look great. You've hardly changed."

Neither spoke. Neither had to. Both were now synchronized to the last time they saw each other and careened toward that memory.

CHICAGO

Claire never did tell Terrie when Frank got married. It was never mentioned among the girls. Now the focus was on Claire and Danny's wedding in a few months. The three girls agreed to be bridesmaids. It was during the selection for their dresses at the bridal shop that Terrie brought up the subject.

"Is he coming?"

"Who? Oh, ah, yeah, him," Claire responded while fingering the material of one of the dresses. "Yes, he is coming and bringing the missus. At least that's what he told Dan. The invitations haven't gone out yet. He said they wouldn't miss it for the world."

"Enough said," Terrie said. "Don't worry, Claire. I'm fine. It's been a few years since I've seen him. I'll be fine. I actually think I'm over him."

"Over who?" Jane piped in, carrying one of the dresses.

Claire looked over at Jane, wide-eyed.

"Oh, him. Ter, you had to know you'd meet up with him somewhere, sometime."

"I was hoping they moved out of the state, or better yet, out of the country. But, I'm fine. Really. It was a silly infatuation. I'm over it."

Claire and Jane exchanged looks, both hoping it was true.

Terrie knew it wasn't true. As her life went on, she thought of him less and less, the memories coming only when she heard certain songs, in particular, a song from Jackson Browne or Traffic. Occasionally a small part of her fantasized on a chance meeting with him where he would profess his feelings for her and the regret he felt for marrying what's-her-name. When she did go out on the occasional date, that person had to match up to her picture of Frank, despite herself.

She told herself the only reason that she ever thought of him at all was that she was still alone and at times, admittedly, lonely. Nancy and Jane occasionally had men in their lives. Terrie's reeked of solitude.

It was at the rehearsal dinner that she finally asked Claire if Frank RSVPed.

"Yes, they did. Both coming."

Terrie tried to hide the emotion she felt but failed.

"You *are* still showing up, right? I mean, you are a bridesmaid," Claire said, seeing the expression on Terrie's face.

"Yes, I'll be there. I promise," Terrie answered with a forced smile. "I'll be fine. It shouldn't bother me. It's just silly after all this time. I'll be okay. No big deal."

"Yeah, right."

"I mean it. Tomorrow is all about you."

When the time came, Terrie made a point not to scan the faces of the people that entered the church and to focus on the ceremony.

Even after the pictures were taken and the reception began, she continued to force herself to ignore the people who were now in the receiving line of the hotel's dining hall. Instead, she headed for the bar, with Nancy and Jane at her side. Terrie faced the opposite direction of the receiving line.

After ordering drinks, she asked her friends, "Alright, Nance, Jane, tell me, are they here?"

"No, oh wait," Nancy replied.

"Oh shit. There he is," Jane said.

Terrie reached for the nearest chair and sat.

"Damn. He does look good in that suit. Black becomes him," Nancy said.

"Is he alone? Is she with him? Girls, tell me."

"He appears to be alone. Maybe she's in the bathroom," Jane said.

"He's walking away. I'm going to ask Claire."

Before she had a chance, Claire looked over at them and motioned the number one.

"Terrie, he's alone," Jane said.

"What?" Terrie responded.

Nancy answered "He came alone. But I must warn you, he looks damn good."

"Now stand up and take a look. Wait, have a drink first."

Terrie did as told.

It was a jolt. A familiar jolt that came so often when she saw him. For a brief second, she wondered if her heart would restart.

"Oh, girls." It came out as a moan. "How am I going to get through this?"

"Crap," Jane said. "Here we go again."

It was Nancy who forced the issue.

"Let's go say hi and get this over with. Are you able to walk?"

"I'm fine. Just give me a minute."

After another gulp of her drink, and with her friends on either side of her, they walked in his direction, where he stood talking to a small cluster of his buddies.

He stopped mid-sentence when he saw them coming. His eyes zoomed in on Terrie. She felt a charge of something she couldn't describe.

"Damn, I think something just happened," Jane muttered to Nancy.

"He doesn't even know we're standing next to her."

Terrie never could remember what was said, something innocuous and inane, but she knew what she felt. No one was going to tear her away from him for the rest of the evening.

But that was short-lived, as she was prodded along to the bridal table. He sat at a nearby table with his friends from the neighborhood. But glances and small smiles were exchanged as the speeches and the meal went on.

Once the music started and she was able to break away from the bridal table, she headed in his direction. The other three girls exchanged glances and shrugged.

"This isn't going to end well," Claire said to the other two.

"Whatever happens, we help her get through it. Agreed?" Nancy said.

"Agreed," the other two replied.

"She has such a determined look on her face," Nancy said.

"How drunk is she?" Jane asked.

"She was putting down a lot of Champaign," Claire said.

"I don't think he's in any better shape," Nancy said.

"I don't suppose there's any way of getting her away from him," Claire said.

"Want your eyeballs ripped out?" Jane said.

"Doesn't help that he's so receptive," Nancy said.

"And so good to look at in that suit," Jane added.

"Well, off to do my bride stuff. Keep me updated," Claire said.

As the music continued, the girls got into the party mood. Between drinking, dancing and meeting up with old friends, they tried to keep an eye on Terrie and Frank.

When the time came to cut the cake, Nancy tugged on Jane's arm.

"I saw her walk out. She got on an elevator."

"Having this wedding in a hotel doesn't help. Damnit. Where's he?"

"I don't see him anywhere," Nancy said. "Oh wait, there he is. Shit. He's heading for the door."

The two girls followed him. They watched him as he caught the next elevator.

"Oh God, Terrie, have you lost your mind?" Nancy whined.

"I guess she has to get this out of her system. Hope she doesn't have any delusions about him leaving his wife. That rarely happens. He's just getting lucky."

"The bastard."

"Don't tell Claire."

"No, I won't. She doesn't need the distraction."

"I'm glad that we're all staying here. Terrie's going to need us to talk her down come morning."

"Nothing we could do now. Let's go enjoy Claire's wedding."

"Yeah, whatever happens, happens."

Terrie looked over at Frank and smiled as they both worked to slow their heartbeats and catch their breath. The sex, passionate and protracted, left them spent.

"It was wonderful, Frank," she murmured. "I don't want this night to ever end."

He looked over at her, gave her a half smile and said nothing.

"This should have happened a long time ago. We belong together," she added.

"Terrie, please. Don't say anything. Not yet. Let's just not talk."

"Fine with me." She rolled over to him, tightly wrapped her arm around him, and planted a kiss on his shoulder.

But she couldn't remain silent for long.

"We have to figure something out."

He mumbled his response.

"Whadya mean? Figure what out?"

"When will I see you again? I have my own place and it's not that far from where you work."

She felt the sudden tension grab hold of him. He gently moved her aside and sat on the side of the bed facing away from her.

"It can't happen again."

"What can't happen? What are you saying, Frank? This was no one night-stand."

"I had too much to drink. So did you."

"That's ridiculous. I saw how you looked at me. I saw that look so many times. Don't tell me this didn't mean something to you."

He began to get dressed.

"Frank, don't you dare get dressed and walk out on me. Talk to me."

"I like you a lot, probably too much," he replied. "I shouldn't have done this." I'm married. I never cheated on her before. This will kill her if she finds out. Yeah, I'm attracted to you. But I'm married to Shelly."

"You can't be serious," Terrie knew she was sounding frantic and didn't care. "I don't want to hear this."

She covered her ears.

"I'm sorry, Terrie. I really am. I don't know what came over me. I shouldn't have done this. It's wrong."

"No, Frank. It's not wrong. It's not. I'm in love with you. I always have been. Since the day I met you."

"Don't say that," he snapped.

"It's true. And you feel the same way. I know you do. I can feel it."

"You're great, Terrie. You really are. But this can't happen again. I can't hurt Shelly. I love her."

Terrie watched as he finished dressing, panic and pain searing her.

"Frank, please. This is real."

"Terrie, stop. There's someone out there for you. It's not me. I'm sorry. I shouldn't have let this happen. I'm so sorry."

"Frank, please don't leave. Let's talk. Please don't go."

He looked at her and said nothing.

"Frank, please," Terrie, now in tears, pleaded. "Don't go."

He kissed her on the forehead and walked from the room.

The rest of Terrie's night was spent veering from dejection, to heartbreak, to rage. She packed and left the hotel before the sun came up, too humiliated to face anyone, even her best friends.

PRESCOTT

Frank looked across the desk at Terrie. Their eyes met.

"Would you like me to go to another bank?" he asked softly.

With a shaking voice, Terrie said, "Don't be silly. It was a long time ago."

"You sure?"

"Yes, I'm sure. Let's get this checking account opened for you," she tried to say brightly as she turned to her computer screen.

He signed his documents and Terrie recited the usual information about the new account.

"Uh, do you," he stammered.

"Do I what?"

"Do you think you'd like to meet for lunch or a drink sometime?"

Terrie looked away.

"It would be nice to catch up on everything and everyone," he added. "I don't know too many people in this town. I certainly don't know anyone from the old neighborhood."

She looked back at him, feeling the familiar jolt.

"Yeah, that would be nice. I'd like that. Here's my card. Call me. I'll, um, meet you somewhere."

He gave her that very familiar smile.

"You can bring your daughter. I'd like to meet her."

Terrie smiled back and said nothing. She watched as he walked away and out through the glass doors.

She walked over to the window and watched him as he got in his car.

"Yes, Frank. I'll bring my daughter. It's time she met her father."

A LITTLE BROWN SHOE

The adults called it muggy. It was a muggy Saturday night. Thick hot air enveloped the night. The rank smell from the stock yards a part of it.

The lights and sounds of the police car and the ambulance cut through it all, as did the pitiful laments of the mother whose little boy lay in the street.

Five-year-old Sophie clung to her mother's dress, her thumb in her mouth. She could see nothing from her vantage point. A crowd of muttering adults encircled her. Looking up, the flickering of the colored lights enthralled her. She felt like she was in a fantasy forest made of tall people and flashing lights.

Sounds floated around her—quivering adult voices in conversations about little Algis. Little Algis was hit by a car. Little Algis was being put into the ambulance. It seemed to the adults around her that it was very bad for little Algis and his mom and dad.

Sophie played with little Algis. They were in the same kindergarten class. She liked little Algis.

Suddenly Sophie was scared and wrapped the hem of her mother's dress tighter in her hand. It was when she looked down that she saw the shoe—a little brown shoe. She picked it up. It confused her. What was a shoe doing on the sidewalk? Where was the other shoe? She wanted to ask someone but didn't. She clung to the shoe.

Her mother picked her up and took her back into their flat. Her mother was crying, so she knew better than to ask questions. When her mother put her in bed she hugged Sophie so tightly that Sophie could barely breathe.

She fell asleep clutching the little brown shoe.

The next day, Sophie put the little brown shoe in her little purse. The little purse usually held some of her favorite crayons, bits of colored paper, and one of her mother's earrings.

The conversation that next morning between her mother, grandmother, and aunt was about poor Algis. He died.

Sophie knew what it meant when someone died. Her daddy died and was with the angels. He was watching over her and keeping her safe. Maybe Algis didn't have anyone who died and was watching over him.

She didn't want Algis to be dead. She liked Algis. He was nice and fun to play with.

It made her sad and no one seemed to notice.

That afternoon, Sophie's mom took her by her hand and said that they were going to visit Algis's mother and father who were so very sad that Algis died. Sophie was told to be a good girl. She nodded to her mother and said that she would be a good girl.

When they walked into the flat of Algis's mother and father, there were other people there. Algis's sister and brother sat on the sofa. To Sophie, they both looked afraid.

Algis's mother was wiping her eyes. His father looked down at the floor and said nothing, not even to the people who stood around him.

Sophie saw the priest from church. She had never seen a priest outside of church. She wanted him to pray for a miracle and bring little Algis back.

Her mother cried as she spoke to Algis's mother.

When her mother stepped aside, Sophie approached Algis's mother. She reached into her little purse, removed the shoe and handed it to her. Sophie didn't know what to say so she said nothing. Algis's mother took the shoe and began to cry. She hugged Sophie. Before Sophie stepped away, she wiped the tears from Algis's mother's cheeks and smiled.

"He's our angel now."

"Yes, Sophie, he's our angel now."

Sophie looked over at her mother, who was smiling at her. She took her mother's hand and they left the flat.

LAST MAN STANDING

The old man let out a grunt as he struggled to stand. He steadied himself on the loose wooden railing that was a part of what was left of the front porch. The action was made more difficult because in one hand he clasped the letter that held the details of his brother's death. He didn't want to damage it. Since he had no phone, it was a Special Delivery letter. The type of letter that held important, but usually bad news.

Once upright, he slowly walked around his property. The dahlias were in bloom and the climbing rose that covered the outhouse was a blaze of deep red, much to the amusement of his fellow farm neighbors, who every year reminded him that he had the best-smelling outhouse in Michigan.

He looked at the small house and shook his head, as he had many times before. The house that his parents built. The house he ran roughshod through with his three brothers so many years ago. For such a small house, you sure hold a lot of memories, he said to the house.

A house now wrapped in washed-out shades of gray and ochre shingles was once bright white with yellow trim. The poorly patched roof now failed to keep out the rainwater. Cardboard and tape covered a window that had been his parents' room. Over the years he joked that the decades-old newspapers and magazines, stacked in all the rooms, probably kept the house standing. The original wood burning stove his mother once cooked on provided his heat and cooked his food. He lived his life in only two of the four rooms. He shared those two rooms with his two aging dogs and piles of books.

Rudy lived a solitary life. A well-informed but solitary life. When not working on his land, he was in the small library of his town. His money was spent on food for him and his dogs. He always managed to own at least two. An equal amount of his funds was spent on newspapers and magazines. A good argument with a local resident over politics or religion made his day, much to their aggravation. In this Christian community, he boasted that he was an atheist. In this rural conservative Republican district, he argued liberal and Democratic politics.

To his face many of his neighbors referred to him as a hermit. He would laugh and tell them to look up the definition of the word. "I'm not a hermit," he would shoot back. "I just don't like most people."

Now, as he stood on his small plot of land, surrounded by his flowers, his vegetable garden, and his house—now a pitiful reminder of what it once was—he opened the letter and read it again.

He looked up at the pure blue sky and thundered.

"God damn you, Stanley! God damn you!" he screamed out the grief that coursed through his worn-out body, "I told you I didn't want to be the last man standing! I told you! Damn you, Stanley, damn you. I told you."

Spent, he fell to his knees, and hung his head.

Rudy's parents, Martha and Józef got married a month before they left their war-torn, shattered village in Poland for the United States. World War One had laid waste to many parts of Poland. Thousands either died fighting in the war or were deported, suspected of collaborating with the enemy. They witnessed the terror and suffering first-hand.

But America—in America there was refuge and safety. There was peace. And, it was said, if you worked hard you had a chance for a good life.

It was a bittersweet occasion. Martha loved Józef but at the age of sixteen she was leaving her parents and her sister, not knowing if they would ever see each other again. They never did. Józef had brothers in Chicago waiting for him. They worked at the stockyards. Filthy work, but it was a start. They would get him a job.

Halfway into the arduous journey, as they crossed the seemingly endless expanse of water, Martha began getting sick. At first, they thought it was seasickness, but she had been fine until then. It wasn't until after they arrived at Ellis Island that she found out she was pregnant. The doctor doing the required physical examination before entry informed the Polish translator who informed Martha.

Edward was born after one of Martha's shifts at the stockyards, in the bedroom of the little cold flat that they shared with another family. Józef was at work when it happened. When he got home, reeking of the odor that followed all the workers from the slaughterhouse, he vowed, to her and his son, that they would leave the filthy, crowded city and get a small farm in the country.

Józef came from a family of farmers in Poland. There wasn't much about farming that he didn't know. So he found odd jobs for the one day that he had off. Martha left Edward with one of the Polish ladies in the neighborhood and went back to work at the stockyards. Between that and the deprivations that they endured, they began to save money. By the time John was born, two years later, they had enough for a down payment on forty acres in Michigan. Józef's brother found someone in the Polish community who had done well financially to lend them the rest. Three per cent interest for ten years. Józef and Martha were elated. Now they just had to build a house and plant the crops.

The house came up with the aid and expertise of Józef's brothers. The crops came up with the aid and expertise of Józef. By the time Rudy was born, two and a half years after John, they were making a little money selling eggs and chickens as well as the crops that they planted. During the winter months, Józef found work in town at a tool and dye factory. They were by no means affluent, but they were getting by and the boys were growing up healthy and strong. When Stanley came along, three years later, he was welcomed by a group of loud and raucous older brothers.

Aside from missing her family in Poland, Martha was happy. She had found the peace and security she needed. She adored her husband and her boys.

Józef and the boys had acclimated to the area. Most of the neighbors and the townspeople had never met anyone from Poland. These were 3rd and 4th generation Michigan farmers, who rarely went to large cities. It took a while for the suspicions and prejudices to abate. It helped that Martha and Josef learned English as well as they did.

The family went to the Catholic Church in town and the boys did well at school. Martha learned to bake on the wood burning stove and always had little Polish pastries to share with the neighbors. It was known that both Martha and Józef were there for anyone going through good times and bad.

December 7, 1941—they heard the news on the radio in their small four-room house. Edward had just turned 21. John was 19 when they both, without hesitation, enlisted. Edward joined the army, John the navy. Rudy was 16 but promised as soon as he was old enough, he would join them. Little Stan, as he was called, echoed his brother's feelings. Józef remained stalwart. He understood. This country had been good to them. It was their duty. Martha could only remember the horrors that World War One inflicted on her native country and wept silently as the boys prepared to leave.

A year and a half later, on a beautiful June day, when the dahlias were in full bloom, Rudy and Stan were working in the corn field when they heard a sound that they would remember for the rest of their lives. It was a wail and it came from their mother. They dropped what they were doing and ran towards the house. When they got there, they froze. Two military men stood in front of their house. One wore a chaplain's collar. Both men looked sad and helpless. Rudy's mother was kneeling on the front porch, beating her chest and rocking backward and forward.

"Not my Eddy!" she screamed. "No! No! Not my Eddy!

"Not my Eddy! Not my Eddy!" She chanted as the sobs broke through. "Not my Eddy!"

Their father stood silently, hands at his side. He stared at his wife, emotionless.

Rudy moved first. Slowly going over to his mother, he helped her to her feet and brought her inside past the two men standing there. There was no need for words.

His father finally spoke. He told Stan to go get the neighbor ladies and the priest. His mother would need them. He then turned and went into the barn.

The mortar blast from the battle in North Africa that took Eddy's life left no remains of Eddy to be buried. But Martha and Józef,insisted on a funeral. They bought a pine coffin. They filled it with Eddy's possessions—his baseball mitt, books he liked, pictures, his favorite cap he wore as a little boy—whatever the four of them could think of. They had a mass said. Almost everyone in town attended. They had a private family funeral at the little cemetery down the road. With his two brothers and uncles as pallbearers they symbolically buried their oldest son. A tombstone with an American flag carved on it went up so that Martha would have a grave to tend. She would then have a photograph of the headstone sent to her family in Poland, even though she didn't know what became of them. It had been over a year since she heard from them.

Thirteen months later, it was a telegram handed to Józef by the parish priest. Martha fainted. Józef, wailed. Rudy screamed at him to go away.

Since John went down with his ship in the Pacific, they had to repeat the funeral process again. Again, no body, just bits and pieces of a short lifetime in a pine box. Martha's eyes took on a haunted, vacant look that she never lost.

Rudy and Stan did not have to serve. The government decided that the family gave enough to their country.

A year after the war officially ended, Rudy was at work on the roof of the barn. Stan was at the bank in town. Martha was in the house jarring tomatoes. Rudy heard a crash. He looked out over the field to see that Józef, had driven his tractor into a tree. His father was slumped over the steering wheel. He ran as fast as he could but knew what he would find. It was his turn to wail as he held his father.

"Don't go, Pa. Please don't go. I need you Pa. Don't go," he sobbed. "I love you Pa. Don't go, please." When the tears subsided, he laid his father on the ground and went to get his mother. This time there would be a body to bury.

Rudy didn't know that you could go mad with grief until he saw it happen to his mother. Within months, Martha's hair turned white. She was in her mid-forties. She spoke Polish to her dead husband as if he was there. She rarely spoke English anymore. Rudy watched her as she cooked enough food for six people. They began taking food to the neighbors. Rudy knew it wouldn't be much longer for her. He was right. She simply didn't wake up one morning. It was the anniversary of Eddy's death.

It was Stan's dream to move to Chicago. He hated farming and wanted to work in an office where you didn't get dirt under your nails. A place where you could wear a suit instead of overalls.

Stan was good with numbers from an early age. As a teen, it was Stan who took over the family books for the farm. His grades in school were always the best of the four brothers. When the opportunity for a correspondence class in accounting came his way, Stan took it.

"Go, Stan. Get a normal life. There is too much pain here," Rudy told his brother, exhausted from grief. "Too many ghosts here,"

"What about you? What are you going to do?" Stan replied. "You can't manage this place by yourself."

"The Colsons down the road are looking for more land," Rudy said "I figure I'll rent out about twenty acres to them. Keep a little for myself. Keep the house. I'll be alright. I think I'll get into the car repair business. You know I love tinkering with engines. I could make a few bucks repairing cars and tractors around here. Anything with a motor."

They gazed at the sun glowing off the cornfield across the road. Neither spoke for a while.

"Go marry that girl in Chicago that you've been writing to," continued Rudy. "The one Uncle Pete fixed you up with. What's her name?"

"Harriet," Stan replied. "I ain't got much to offer her though."

"Like I said, go to Chicago. We got all those relatives out there. You could stay with one of them until you get a job at a bank or something."

"I hate leaving you," Stan admitted.

"I hate that you have to leave. But you know me. I love this farm. Hate the city. What else do I know? Besides, ma and pa went through a lot to get this place. They gave us a good home. I can't walk away from it. I just can't. But you can. One of us has to go out and get married and have kids and it ain't gonna be me. I could tell you that for sure."

Stan nodded, unable to speak.

A week later the arrangements were made.

"Take good care of yourself little brother," Rudy said to Stan as they stood in the driveway. "I don't want to be the last man standing."

Stan looked away, afraid that Rudy might see the tears in his eyes.

"Either do I, big brother. So you do the same," he finally said. The two brothers hugged, then Stan got in the car and drove away.

As he stood there and watched his brother's car fade into the dust, he vowed he would not love anyone again. It hurt too much when they left you behind.

A WEDDING

It was a day that many of the people in the neighborhood had been looking forward to. The eldest daughter of the family that owned the corner bar was getting married.

They were a family of means, so expectations were high. In the midst of the Depression, a grand wedding was eagerly anticipated, especially by the women and girls in the neighborhood.

The daughter, Birute, called Ruth by her friends, was not only pretty but hard-working as well. She worked at a factory that made tin cans. The groom, Peter, was also well-liked. He held a good job in the office of the Armour Company over by the stockyards. They would have a good future together.

Ruth's parents owned the building that housed the bar and the apartments above it. They also owned the house next to this building, which is where they lived with their two daughters and two sons. Ruth was the first in the family to get married.

The reception would be held in the tavern's back hall. The word was out that the tavern would be closed that day, with an open bar available to the invitees of the wedding.

No expense was spared. The neighbors watched as dozens of floral arrangements were delivered to the church and the hall.

The best cooks in the area were hired to prepare the wedding feast. The guests would be assured a dinner with not only the best roast beef and chicken, but seemingly endless dishes of pierogis and kugelis.

The ladies at the little nearby bakery said that they were working on the largest and most beautiful of wedding cakes.

The best polka band in the area was hired. The music as important as the food.

The pastor of the church would officiate the wedding mass. All the lights in the huge church would be lit, as they would be for a high mass or a major Holy Day like Easter.

It was said that 150 people were invited, which included the precinct captain and his family as well as the police captain. It was a large gathering for that neighborhood. Those lucky to get an invitation bragged about it as they shopped for new dresses and suits.

The wedding was on a perfect May day—bright sunshine and a cloudless sky.

When the bride stepped out of her house, followed by her six bridesmaids and a flower girl, she was met with applause and cheers by the folks gathered around waiting for this moment. She smiled and waved. She was helped into the car by her bridesmaids and laughed as she tried to make room for her father. The dress and veil seemed to take up all the space.

Both sides of the aisle in the church held large groups of people, probably the most ever for a wedding at this church.

Once the organist began to play, all faces turned to the back of the church to see Ruth on her father's arm. Both with eyes glowing as they smiled at the crowd.

Ruth's dress, satin with a lace bodice and sleeves and a six-foot train and veil, brought gasps and even tears.

The lovely bridesmaids and flower girl completed the pageant. A sight many people said they would never forget.

The mass was a bit long, but with all the ceremony and music that was required. It was also unforgettable.

The bride and groom beamed as they came down the aisle. Once outside the church, they were showered with rice.

After going to the photographer's studio for pictures and a short interlude, the newly married couple went over to the hall for the reception.

For days, weeks, even years after, those who attended the wedding were still relating stories of the best wedding that they ever attended. The food, excellent. The beer and whiskey flowed until well past midnight. The dancing was nonstop, with the beat of the polkas and the melodies of the waltzes heard late into the night.

Even those who were not fortunate enough to be invited enjoyed the day, clutching its overflowing remnants. It was the day when the streets were swept almost to a shine by the ladies on each block, the trees were beginning to bloom, and the joy of the newly married couple and their generous family filled the hearts of their neighbors. A day to be remembered.

Twenty-five years later the couple returned to the same church and hall for their anniversary party. They had no children, but the many nieces and nephews and friends seemed enough for the two of them. They had a good life.

As predicted, they did do very well and were very generous with their time and money. They built a large brick home in another neighborhood, but never forgot where they came from, as some people did. They were well known for the many get-togethers that they hosted.

For their fiftieth anniversary, the nieces and nephews arranged the celebration at a popular Lithuanian restaurant. The couple looked as happy then as they did on the day of their wedding. The look of love still shown in their eyes, even after their many years together.

One Sunday they met with several of their friends and family members at St. Casimir's Cemetery to show off the headstone that they had purchased for themselves, already installed and with the dates left blank. A picture taken on their wedding day was placed between their names. Holding hands, they admired the mason's work.

Six years later Peter went first. Three days after his funeral Ruth joined him.

BEING BETTY
1955

Her name was Betty. Behind her back they called her the Back of the Yards Beauty, and she was, what with her perfectly coifed, raven black hair, and color-coordinated outfits. No detail was overlooked. The shoes, the purse, the gloves, the hat, always a perfect match to the suit. If it was a lilac day, she was a vision in lilac from head to toe. If her suit was yellow, she was all in yellow.

On nice mornings, Betty walked to work—a neighborhood bank where she was the secretary to the Vice President. As she walked down the street and passed the tar-shingled two flats and the shabby taverns, she commanded attention. Children, especially the girls, stopped playing just to stare. The old ladies in their drab sweaters and aprons stopped sweeping their sidewalks, in the hope that she would smile at them or stop for a chat. All gossip was suspended until she passed by.

If the weather wasn't suitable, her father or a neighbor would drive her to the bank and pick her up at the end of the day. But it was those mornings she walked to work that she enjoyed the most.

The bank where she worked was the largest in the area. Not far from the stockyards, it was, for many years, the main depository for many of the large accounts coming out of the meat packing industry. Betty's position as the secretary to the vice-president was an important one. She knew someday he would be president, and she would follow him.

Betty graduated at the top of her class at Jones Commercial, a school whose main goal was to refine the girls of Chicago going into the clerical workforce, teaching them not only typing and shorthand but all they needed to know in the way of wardrobe, manners, and a host of subjects. To be in service to these important men was more than a job—it was an honor.

Betty started in a secretarial pool, but was moved up to her position in a matter of months. It didn't take long for Betty to make an impression. The fact that she was having an affair with the vice president also had something to do with her quick rise to the position of his secretary.

An only child, Betty's Lithuanian immigrant parents doted on her. Her father was a foreman at one of the nearby factories and did well for himself. They were one of the few families to own a single-family bungalow and to have a new car almost annually.

It never occurred to her parents to charge Betty rent, so Betty indulged herself with shopping. She shopped mostly at some of the better ladies' apparel shops on Ashland, but at times, she could be seen coming off the streetcar with green packages that carried the Marshall Field's logo. If she didn't appear so pleasant, there would be plenty of snide remarks to go around. She had no close friends and never went to the taverns or to the events in the area. Betty was not about to associate with any of these people, especially the men. Those men in their overalls, with tobacco-stained calloused fingers, who reeked of bad beer repulsed her.

Betty never missed the noon high mass on Sunday at her church. It was an occasion to be seen and for her to talk about her job at the bank with the women who either stayed home with their kids or worked in nearby factories.

Betty never looked at any man as a potential husband. The affair with Stanley, her boss, was enough for Betty. When his wife (who Betty considered a dowdy old cow) was at their summer cottage in Wisconsin with the children (children who Betty could barely tolerate when they showed up at the bank), Betty and Stan checked into the Palmer House as husband and wife.

Any out-of-town meetings that Stan attended always had Betty following him on the next train and checking into another room, a room she hardly stepped into. Otherwise it was the occasional workday evening when he let his staff know that he had to work late and needed his secretary to be there.

If there was office gossip, it was kept quiet. Repeating rumors about the vice president and eventual president would not help anyone's career advancement or even their position as a teller.

This is the life, Betty would think, while sprawled naked next to Stanley. This is what it's all about. Room service, martinis, driving her lover out of his mind with techniques she read about in the naughty magazines. Who needs a husband, kids, housework when you can have all of this?

Betty was never a political person. Her tastes veered more towards fashion magazines and society and gossip columns in the newspapers. That changed the minute she saw Jack Kennedy and his wife on that little black-and-white TV. She was enthralled. More than anything she wanted to see this man become president and Jackie to be First Lady. She even went so far as to volunteer for his campaign. Since everyone in this Catholic, Democrat neighborhood wanted this as well, her job was easy. She bought every magazine and newspaper with photos of the Kennedys that she could get her hands on. She started a scrapbook of clippings and photos. Election Day was one of the most exciting days of her life, second only to the inauguration.

Now when shopping, Betty bought anything that even remotely looked like something Jackie wore. Her hairstyle became a replica of Jackie's, and she wore an identical pillbox hat.

When news came that Kennedy was assassinated, Betty ran from the bank in near hysteria. She wore black for weeks. Her parents could hardly console her. Even Stan, whom she had been seeing less of lately, grew tired of trying to cheer her up.

That following February, her father collapsed on the front stairs, after leaving the tavern across the street. He died instantly. Strangely enough, Betty could hardly shed a tear. It was as if she used them all up for the Kennedys. At the funeral, which she made sure was the grandest one since the pastor of the parish died, Betty wore a black veil similar to the one Jackie wore at her husband's funeral. It almost cheered her up, until she realized that after the condolences and the attention, she would be living solely with her mother.

Betty never liked her mother, Leona, very much. In her estimation, her mother was too old-fashioned, too ingrained in that neighborhood. The fact that her mother wore babushkas and still spoke with a thick Lithuanian accent embarrassed Betty. She liked her father, but was equally embarrassed by him. His Saturday nights in that smelly tavern with those crude, drunken oafs infuriated Betty.

Why didn't they move to California instead of staying in this foul-smelling Back of the Yards, with the dirty air and all the backward, uncouth peasant immigrants? She wanted to be in California, in the warmth, without the gray crusty snow and frigid winter temperatures. She daydreamed about swimming in the ocean, lying on the warm sand on those endless cloudless days. She fantasized about the attention she would garner, especially from men, as she lay on the beach in her skimpy bikini. Of course, the men would be movie stars, lying beside her instead of on a movie screen. The faces would change depending on the latest movie Betty saw. Her room was now filled with the magazines that covered the movies and its stars.

When she was a teenager, the young couple a few doors away were the talk of the neighborhood. They had packed up and moved to Long Beach, California. The older people were aghast. You don't leave your mother, your father, your brothers and your sisters and move so far away. It just wasn't done.

But Betty wanted to leave. Over time her revulsion of the neighborhood increased. In her mind even the children were crude little urchins. What did these people know about life outside this neighborhood? What did they know about downtown Chicago with its nightclubs, hotels and fancy restaurants? What did they know about California? She no longer bothered to speak to the neighborhood women, whom she now considered unsophisticated peasants. It wasn't long before she was labeled a stuck-up by people who once admired her.

Stan may have been married with children and increasingly paunchy and bald, but he showed her the world outside of the Yards. For that she would always be grateful. And for that she always wanted more.

In the weeks and months after her father's funeral, Betty would find herself sitting across the kitchen table listening to her mother's many complaints.

Betty considered her mother a nag. A nag who was never happy with anything her father did. Betty felt this was the reason her father spent as much time as he did in the tavern. But now things were worse. Her mother didn't grieve or even shed a tear for her husband. She was just plain angry; angry that her husband had the nerve to die on her, leaving her with decisions to make and changes to deal with. Betty listened in silence as her mother ranted on about who would cut the grass come spring and who would finish the work that they started on in the basement. Though she received a good insurance settlement, she still repeatedly asked Betty what she was going to do for money.

Before long, Betty knew she had to learn how to drive. Her father's Chevrolet sat in the garage while the walk to work was becoming more inconvenient, especially in bad weather. She took driving lessons and was surprised at how much she enjoyed it. The sense of freedom that driving gave her was offset by her mother's many errands and doctor appointments. Her mother now relied on her more than ever. Betty could feel her mother's voice crawling under her skin. Going to work became an escape from the incessant complaining and pointless small talk.

The days became weeks and then months and soon years, and nothing in Betty's life changed. She still wore the color-coordinated outfits and high heels. She was the most important secretary at the bank since Stan was now president. But it didn't matter. She still attracted the attention of the men who walked in the bank. But that didn't matter either.

Betty was not happy.

The world around Betty changed. She picked up pieces of it on the 6 o'clock news but she chose to ignore it.

It was happening too fast.

It felt as if there were cracks in the foundation of her life—cracks that continued to grow.

There was a war going on somewhere and race riots somewhere else. There was the assassination of Martin Luther King, which spurred riots. Betty couldn't understand why. But then came the assassination of Robert Kennedy. This, Betty could not ignore. She wore the black veil again and wept loudly during mass. And then came the news of Jackie getting married to a Greek billionaire. "Jackie, where is your pillbox hat and the Chanel suit?" Betty asked out loud to the television. There was Jackie in a loose-fitting floral dress and longer hair. "Why are you dressed this way?"

Another crack in her foundation appeared.

And her aging mother aged more rapidly, more loudly, more intrusively.

One humid summer day, she heard her mother cry, "Look. Look at that! Betty, come see!"

Betty raced to the picture window where Leona was standing.

"Isn't that Stella's granddaughter? The one that went to Catholic high school, the one that we all thought would be a nun?" Betty said to her mother.

Betty looked at the girl walking down the street. The girl with the long blond hair, wearing a mini skirt and no, no,...

"She's no wearing bra! She's no wearing bra!" screamed her mother. Betty gasped.

"How could she go out in public looking like that? She looks like a whore! Dear God!" responded Betty. She had heard about girls dressing like this, but this was the first time she saw it. And in this neighborhood yet.

There was something about this girl, this braless girl who she knew as a child, whom she had seen in church over the years wearing a white veil, deep in prayer, that shook Betty and made her to look around. She began to look at the houses on her street and the businesses in her neighborhood.

Nothing was the same. Her mother often carried on about the people who were moving out of the neighborhood and the Mexicans that were moving in. But Betty blocked it out with her mother's other complaints. She was told that an Arab family was buying the grocery store on the corner. That made even less sense to Betty. Her mother must be losing her mind. Why would an Arab family come here? Why would an Arab family leave the sunny exotic desert and come to this dismal old neighborhood? A madness permeated the air.

Betty walked into her bedroom and looked at her surroundings. She looked at the same chenille bedspread that had been on her bed for years. She glared at the same furniture, lamps and wall color. She ran her hands over the clothes in her closet that had remained the same despite the changing styles. It was all the same but suddenly different.

She sat down on her bed as she felt the foundation cracks grow even larger. She became afraid that she would be devoured by the cracks that were becoming more real to her every day.

It was time to go.

One Saturday, she went across the street to see her neighbor, Vicki. Vicki's husband recently died, and Betty feared that she too might move away, especially since her only son had moved to the suburbs. She was a good friend to Betty's mother. They had known each other from their teenage years.

Vicki told Betty that she had no intention of leaving.

"I'm staying put. This is the house I was born in. This is my neighborhood. I'm not going nowhere, and my kid knows that. I don't care about the Mexicans or the Arabs. They don't bother me," she told Betty.

Relieved, Betty told her that she was going on a vacation and asked Vicki if she could spend a couple of hours a day with her mother. This included running errands and taking her to the doctor. Betty offered to pay her a hundred dollars a week, an amount Vicki was not about to turn away.

"Where are you going to? It's the end of October, too cold for Wisconsin," Vicki asked.

"California. With a friend of mine. We're going to California," was Betty's reply.

"How wonderful! When are you going? When will you be back?"

"I'm not sure. We're driving. I'm sure we'll be back in a couple of weeks. I have so much vacation time at the bank, I may as well use it up before the holidays," Betty said with a smile.

"I haven't told my mother yet. I need to work out the details, so please don't say anything yet."

"Okay, my lips are sealed until you tell me it's okay," Vicki said, grinning at their little conspiracy.

"Thank you, Vicki." Betty said. "Thank you."

The following Monday, Betty called in sick. It was the first time that she ever called in sick when she wasn't.

"Why you not going to work? You no sick," Leona yelled. Since her hearing had faded in recent years, she yelled all of her conversations at Betty. She also reverting to speaking every other phrase in Lithuanian, which irritated Betty even more.

"I have things to do," Betty replied.

"What things? And what the hell is wrong with you hair? Now a funny color. You go see Cecelia and get it fixed? It look like crap."

"I'm not coloring it for a while. I want a new look," Betty said, staring out the window.

"It look like crap. And where the hell you goin'?" she said when she saw Betty putting on her jacket.

"I won't be gone long."

"What you saying? Where you going?" was the last rant that Betty heard her mother yell as she slammed the door and walked to the car.

When she returned a couple of hours later, she was driving a yellow Volkswagen beetle.

This time there was no getting Leona to stop the bellowing.

"What the hell that thing? You go crazy? You get rid of your father's beautiful car for that piece of garbage?"

And on it went throughout the rest of the day and evening.

"It's better on gas." "The Chevy was falling apart." Nothing Betty said could calm her mother down.

Until she finally screamed—"I need it for my trip to California!"

"What trip? You go crazy or what? You sick?"

"I'm leaving in a couple of weeks to go on a vacation to California with a friend from work. I need a vacation. I'm not even going to try to explain. I know you won't understand."

With that Betty went into her room and closed the door. She blasted the radio and let Nat King Cole block the Lithuanian cursing coming from the other side of the door. Then she walked over to her dresser, took out a pair of scissors, slowly cut her chenille bedspread into small strips, and left them in a pile on the floor.

That following Friday, at the end of the workday, she stopped at the teller window and withdrew a large amount of cash. She then left a properly typed envelope on Stan's desk, walked out of the bank, and drove home.

Smiling, she realized that the cracks were sealing. There would be no descent into a chasm.

She walked in the house to find her mother sitting in the kitchen, waiting for Betty to make dinner. She was getting the silent treatment, which suited Betty just fine. After dinner, Betty prepared her mother's tea with an addition of sleeping pills. They worked quickly. While her mother slept on the couch, Betty went downstairs and retrieved her one piece of luggage and a travel case. From a bag in her room, she brought out the first pair of jeans she ever owned and a road atlas.

After packing, she put on the jeans. They were going to take some getting used to, but when she saw herself in the mirror, she smiled. She then sat down and wrote two notes—one for her mother and one for Vicki. Vicki's included several hundred dollars with a promise of more to come. The note to her mother briefly stated that she went on vacation to California. She included a fifty-dollar bill.

Her mother was snoring, and the television was blaring when Betty went to the kitchen and made coffee. While the coffee brewed, she went out to put the note in Vicki's mailbox. Her note to her mother went on the kitchen counter. Once her thermos was filled, she grabbed her purse and suitcases, then loaded up her little car. Without turning around or a moment of hesitation, she drove away. A bystander would have seen a smile on her face.

The postcards started coming in the following weeks. Initially from Missouri, then somewhere in Texas, then two from Santa Fe. They said very little— "Lovely mountains" or "having a great time"

"It's almost Thanksgiving. When she come back?" her mother would ask Vicki. Vicki found herself spending more time with her friend then she bargained for. She had forgotten how difficult this woman could be.

"Why don't she call? What the hell going on? She's gonna lose her job at the bank." This was the refrain Vicki heard daily. Vicki knew she missed her daughter but would never admit it. She continued to chastise Betty even though she wasn't even in the state, much less the room.

Two weeks before Christmas, a postcard from Long Beach, California—a postcard with a picture of Santa wearing shorts. Still no indication of when she would be returning. "Having a wonderful time!" was all it said.

When Vicki finally did get a letter, it was on Christmas Eve. There was a note and a couple of hundred dollars. There was also a picture of a blond-haired woman in a bikini, clinging to a man with hair down to his shoulders. One arm wrapped around the woman, the other around a surfboard. The beach in the background. It came from a place called Venice Beach. The note simply said, "Merry Christmas! From Betty."

Vicki trudged across the street to show the picture to Leona. She didn't think she could make her friend understand what was happening. She didn't understand it herself.

"That's not her. You're crazy. When is she coming back? You no telling me the truth. Where the hell is she? Who is this woman in this picture?" groaned Betty's mother.

"It's Betty, Leona. It's Betty."

For the first time, Vicki saw fear in her friend's eyes.

"This make no sense. She has everything here. I'm her mama. What happened? What happened to my girl?"

Vicki sat down wearily. She looked at the small Christmas tree with presents underneath that Leona had bought for her daughter. Then they both quietly watched the snow as it fluttered down, the picture in Leona's shaking hand.

Two thousand miles away, early in the morning of that same Christmas Eve, Betty stood on the pier at Seal Beach and looked out at the ocean, the wind blowing through her straight blond hair.

"Merry Christmas California!" she said loudly. "I'm all yours. Ain't no going back."

With that Betty turned and walked quickly toward the little clothing boutique where she now worked.

EDDIE AND CHESTER

Chester sat on the rickety, worn bench that his grandfather had roughly assembled and plunked in front of their two-flat house. He counted his pennies again. This was the best game of lagging that he ever had. He won enough for a bag of chips and a Pepsi. Yeah, it was a good day.

He thought back to the game. The annoyed looks of his fellow players whose pennies he now held made him smile. It was a simple game. You flipped your pennies from a short distance away toward the crack in between the sidewalk sections. Whoever got the closest, better yet, had his pennies land directly on the crack, was the winner and claimed all the pennies.

This accounted for Chester's financial windfall. It was his second big win this week. Not bad for this twelve-year-old kid. He knew he should put the pennies in his bank in his bedroom, but the thought of that Pepsi, ice cold and frothy on this hot summer day, prevented him from making such a responsible move.

He got up, shoved the pennies in the pocket of his jeans, wiped his hands on his shirt and headed for the grocery store across the street. He stopped short when a car pulled up in front of him. It wasn't just any car. It was a souped up '58 Ford, bright red and loud. A Chuck Berry song burst through the windows. Stepping out from the passenger side came Eddie.

Chester grinned from ear to ear when he saw Eddie. Eddie with the slicked back, Brylcreamed ducktail, the black jeans and tight white tee-shirt, a pack of Lucky Strikes encased in the left sleeve. Eddie—the coolest guy on the block and Chester's friend.

"Hey, Chester," Eddie addressed the young boy. "How's it going, kid?"

The beaming Chester forgot about his Pepsi and went into an enthusiastic version of how he beat his buddies in lagging pennies for a second time.

Eddie listened and acted impressed. He reached in his pocket and pulled out a nickel.

"Here ya go. Next time play for the big bucks."

"Gee, thanks, Eddie. I will. Thanks."

Chester was still smiling as he watched Eddie walk into the gangway leading to his flat.

Wait till I tell the guys, he thought, knowing that they would be impressed that someone as cool as Eddie was Chester's buddy and even gave him a nickel.

Chester lived upstairs from Eddie with his parents and older sister. The building was owned by his parents. The downstairs consisted of yet another neighborhood tavern. The tavern and the flat behind it was being rented by Eddie's father, Ed senior. When young, Eddie was referred to as Junior, but it wasn't long before he announced that his name was Eddie. Any kid calling him Junior would get a punch in his arm bad enough that they would never call him Junior again.

Chester once asked his father why Eddie didn't have a mother.

She died, he was told, when Eddie was a baby. Don't bring it up.

The day Eddie announced to his father that he was dropping out of school, Chester could hear the shouts coming up from the thin walls. His father, a Lithuanian immigrant who fled the Soviets and the aftermath of the Second World War just ten years before, wanted his son to get a good American education, followed by a good job.

But Eddie had other plans. Eddie was in a gang. Not just any gang, but the Saints, considered one of the toughest in the area. Eddie had the look, the swagger and the one essential—a switchblade.

When not working with his father in the tavern, Eddie could be found on a street corner or at the nearby park huddled with his fellow gang members, smoking, spitting, and glaring squint-eyed at anyone who looked in their direction.

The girls got the Elvis raised eyebrow and a mumbled remark. Blushing and giggling, the girls would slowly walk away.

To his father's shame, Eddie was considered a juvenile delinquent by some of the people in the neighborhood—a criminal—a hood.

Others, usually the older men sitting on stools in the tavern considered Eddie and the others as boys impatient to be men. Put them in an Army uniform and tell them to shoot the Germans or the Japs, like we had to, and they'll see how tough they really are.

Eddie and his fellow gang members heard this talk and mocked the older men and their gossipy wives. They were tougher than any of these old folks knew. They were protecting not only their turf, but the neighborhood from the non-whites—the Mexicans, the Puerto Ricans, the Blacks. They were looking after their own people. If it meant a rumble, so be it. Someone had to do it. Someone had to take a stand.

Chester spent a lot of time downstairs in Ed's Tavern. His parents were there most Friday and Saturday evenings with the neighbors. The kids were welcome as long as they behaved themselves. After they bought the kids their Pepsis and chips they turned away—the women to nurse their highballs and gossip, the men to hover over their boilermakers, getting loud over discussions of their jobs, the White Sox or Daley politicians.

If he could collect a couple of dimes, Chester played the bowling game while the girls played their favorite songs on the jukebox and jitterbugged. Everly Brothers and Elvis Presley the obvious favorites for his sister and her friends.

When not involved in the bowling game, Chester just watched Eddie. He liked Eddie's unfriendly attitude. It made him feel special that he was one of the few Eddie spoke to. Chester got the smile the others didn't. He got his hair ruffled and a gentle punch on the arm, while others got his cocky, unfriendly attitude.

To his father's wrath, Eddie would often disappear, not to return, even if the place was full of patrons. Ed knew better than to display his anger in front of his customers. He would get no sympathy, just remarks on how he let his kid get away with murder. But Chester saw it. Chester knew where Eddie went. The '58 red Ford would be parked on the corner. He would smile at Eddie. Eddie would nod and wink at Chester before he snuck out the side door. It was their secret.

And Eddie was just the coolest guy in the neighborhood.

Chester had another secret.

Once summer came, the shingled flats absorbed and relentlessly clung on to the brutal humidity and heat that saturated the Chicago air. The small portable fans did little to alleviate the situation. Sleeping became a task. Some people chose to sleep on back porches. Others who lived near tree-lined boulevards or a park would gather their families and sleep outdoors beneath trees on the cool grass, only to wake covered with mosquito bites.

Chester would wait until he knew his parents were asleep, his father's snoring an indication. He would wet a towel, place it around his neck and very quietly leave the flat. He would sit on his grandfather's bench and watch the night. It became a ritual for him. Even nights that were cooler because of rain, Chester still went out and sat on the bench.

He loved the sudden solitude. No screeching kids, the tavern dark and silent, no prattling adults who seemed to never run out of conversation. Occasionally a car passed. The lights of the flats out for the night, an occasional unrecognizable sound from an open window, a far-off siren, the grocery store across the street now in total darkness.

He knew it would end when the weather cooled off and it was time to go back to school. It would end if his parents ever found out. Until that time, he would continue this nightly excursion.

He felt safe here, safer than even in his home with his parents, safer than in the daytime, where some voices seemed only inches away from violence.

This night was different. Sirens, there were more sirens. Sirens made the night tense. He wished they would stop.

He looked in both directions. There was a movement when he looked to the left—a sudden movement in the shrubs in front of the house by the alley. A shrouded figure emerged—it rose and fell as it came nearer. It clung for a few moments to the shrubs in front of each house, then moved on.

Chester was afraid. He was never afraid out here before. This wasn't a drunk staggering home from the corner tavern. This shadowy shape was headed in his direction. He gripped the edge of the bench and pressed himself against the wall hoping the creature wouldn't see him. It got nearer. Chester could feel his heart thump in his chest.

It was at the house next door, just feet away. Chester closed his eyes. If he didn't see it, maybe it wasn't there.

The voice came out of nowhere, a whisper.

"Hey, kid, is that you? Chester?"

Chester opened his eyes and relief overtook him.

It was Eddie. Now confusion overtook him. Why was Eddie acting like a frightening creature of the night?

The voice came from the gangway.

"Kid, come here. Quick."

Chester looked around before leaving the bench and headed for Eddie's voice.

Eddie was crouched down in the gangway.

"Hi, Eddie. What's going on?"

"I can ask you the same thing. Why you sitting out here in the middle of the night?"

"Couldn't sleep. Too hot, so I came down here for a while."

"Yeah, okay," Eddie said with a tremor in his voice.

Chester didn't think Eddie even heard him. His breathing was loud, and he smelled bad. In the dim patch of light from the street lamps Chester could make out Eddie's features. Eddie looked scared, his features marred.

"What's a matter, Eddie?" Chester asked in a coarse whisper.

Eddie didn't respond. The sound of his breathing pierced the darkness.

"What's wrong, Eddie?' Chester asked again.

"I need your help, kid. Okay? But you can't tell nobody about it. It's real important. You're like my buddy. Can I count on you to help a pal?"

"Sure, Eddie, sure thing," the boy responded proudly. "What ya need me to do?"

"First off, you can't tell nobody that you saw me."

"Yeah, sure. They think I'm upstairs sleeping. I won't tell."

"I need some money. Can you get me some?"

"Huh? Money?" he replied, bewildered. "Eddie, all I got is my pennies. You can have those. That's all I got."

"I need more than pennies. I need you to go upstairs and find you mother's purse or your ol' man's wallet. Take the cash and bring it down here. I'm going in the bar and see what's in the cash register. He usually leaves something in there."

Chester was stunned into silence. *Stealing is a sin. Stealing from your parents has got to be a mortal sin.*

"I, I dunno, Eddie. What if I get caught? What's up, Eddie? Why do you need the money?"

"The cops are after me."

Chester heard himself gasp. He thought back to the sounds of the sirens tonight.

"Why, Eddie, why are the cops after you? What happened? I don't get it."

"Cuz I hurt someone tonight. I hurt someone bad."

"Did he hurt you? Did you get in a fight?"

"Yeah, kid. We got in a fight. At the park. It wasn't my fault. Lousy spic. It's our turf. He didn't belong there. I didn't see the old lady."

"What old lady?" Chester asked, confused.

"The old lady sleeping by the tree," Eddie replied, suddenly in his own world. It seemed to Chester that he was talking to someone else.

"Why can't people just stay in their own houses? So what if it's hot out? She had no business being there. Sleeping by the goddamned tree. She shoulda been in her bed at home. Not sleeping in the park like a bum."

"By herself?" Chester asked.

"No. Yeah. I don't know. There were other people in the park."

Eddie stopped talking.

"What happened, Eddie? I don't get it. What happened?"

"The lousy Mexican, it was all his fault. He jumped me – tried to beat me up, but I got away. I ran and he was after me, looking for me. He woulda killed me. I had to get him first. I still had my knife."

That was when Chester really noticed Eddie's face. He was bleeding, the blood smearing every time he wiped his face. Chester knew he was smelling blood mixed with sweat and began to tremble.

"Yeah, you had to get him," was all he could say.

"I ran. I was hiding by a tree and the old lady started to scream. She was giving me away. She wouldn't stop screaming. So I stuck her with my knife. I had to shut her up. I had to. The bastard would find me. I had to shut her up."

Chester tried to convince himself that this was just part of a dream. He's fallen asleep on the bench. This was just a dream.

"There were other people there. They all started yelling at me. I ran."

"Why did the Mexican beat you up, Eddie?" Chester asked feebly.

"I was messing around with one of their girls. Little Consuelo. Hot little thing. She was askin for it. Her brother found out. So he came after me. Someone musta called the cops. The sirens are all over the place."

"Yeah, Eddie. They are."

Eddie seemed to snap out of it.

"That's why I need some cash and I need it fast. I'll head downtown and get on the first train or Greyhound out of town. You gotta help me kid. You gotta.

I'll send the money back as soon as I get away and get a job or something. You just gotta help me kid. Ya gotta. I think some of those people in the park knew me. The cops are probably on their way over here now."

Chester stared back mutely until Eddie shook him by the shoulders.

"Get upstairs now and get some cash. I'm going to my ol' man's tavern. Meet ya down here in a coupla minutes," he said as he pushed the boy out of the gangway.

"Go," Eddie ordered. "Now, goddammit."

Chester obeyed. He ran up the stairs to his flat, not sure of what he was doing or why. Suddenly he was afraid of Eddie. When he got to the top of the landing, he stopped long enough to think about what he had to do next.

His father kept his wallet and keys on top of the dresser in their room.

Chester headed for his parent's bedroom. His father was snoring. His mother lay sprawled on her stomach, quietly breathing. On tiptoes, he went over to the dresser, reached for the wallet, and took out the cash. He looked down at the cash. It was eleven dollars. Chester hoped it was enough to get Eddie out of the city. With shaking hands, he put the wallet back on the dresser.

The sirens that were off in the distance were now shrieking. Lights from two squad cars lit up the darkness. They were in front of his house. The boy froze were he stood.

Both parents were suddenly awake. He heard his parents' voices.

"What the hell's going on?" his father muttered.

"I don't know," his mother said, her voice groggy with sleep. "Chester, what are you doing here?"

"What the hell's going on?" His father repeated, as he got out of the bed and headed for the window. "It's the cops. Jesus Christ, there out in front. What the hell."

Both parents threw on robes as they bolted from the room, now oblivious to their son.

All the neighbors appeared to be doing the same thing. A paddy wagon was now part of the commotion.

Chester slowly followed his parents, clutching the eleven dollars in his trembling hands.

He heard one officer bark orders for everyone to stand back. Another, sweaty and brash, threw questions at Chester's father. Chester could hardly breathe.

Then there was Eddie's father, dressed only in his tee shirt and shorts, being shoved toward a squad car by still another cop. Confused and scared, his responses were in Lithuanian. Raucous questions and comments from all directions added to the cacophony swirling around Chester. Someone mentioned a gun.

Where are you Eddie? He almost blurted out loud. *Where are you?* He felt someone push him toward the neighbor's house two doors away. He tried to squirm away. It was his mother's hands digging fiercely into his shoulders.

With his heart pounding furiously in his chest, Chester kept his eyes glued to the gangway where he had last seen Eddie just minutes before.

There were more bellows from the cops and more twitters from the crowd that had gathered.

Then it happened. First there was the cop, looking smug. "Good job, guys." Chester heard him say. He was followed by a handcuffed Eddie and two more cops.

Chester broke from his mother's grip.

"Let him go!" he heard himself shriek. "He didn't do nothing! He was here with me. Let him go!"

Someone had him by the waist. He fought him off with all his strength and ran toward Eddie.

"Chester, it's okay," Eddie looked over his shoulder at Chester as the cops pushed him toward the paddy wagon. "It's gonna be okay. Be cool. Thanks, kid."

It was when the doors of the paddy wagon were slammed shut that the tears came.

"He didn't do nothing! He didn't do nothing!" he yelled. The mantra continued as his father picked him up and carried him upstairs and laid him on his bed.

His parents swirled around him uttering reassurances that meant nothing to him. His sobs subsided, the noises inside and outside of the flat diminished.

Chester lay awake until dawn crept in, the eleven dollars in his pants pocket. The last look from Eddie's face now seared into his brain. The words "Thanks, kid." remained in the air, clear and blistering.

He knew something happened to him that night. It was more than something that would linger as a bad memory.

He lost a part of himself.

IN SILENCE

Tony walked into the tavern expecting it to be different. It wasn't. The same scuffed wooden floor, the same faded cardboard beer ads plastered to the wall—*Hamms Beer - From the Land of Sky Blue Waters*—still in the same spot. The pungent tang of beer and cigarettes still a part of the place, ingrained in the surroundings. The grimy mirror behind the bar still reflected the craggy faces of the men on their stools.

It should be different, he told himself. He was different. Not on the outside. But inside. He knew he would never return to the young man that existed before the war. When you've killed and wounded so many, how could you not be changed? When you escaped death on the battlefield so many times, how can you be untouched? When your very soul has been transformed, do people notice?

The family and friends left behind, they're different too. How could they not be? War scarred everyone that it touched.

But we go through the motions, he thought. We're all pretending that things are the way they were before the war. His mother made the same food. His father had the same job. His sisters still laughed, but with a strain.

If I pretend too, he thought, *maybe I'll feel normal someday*. That's what the counselors at the Veteran's Administration were saying to the returning GIs. "Just act normal and you'll feel normal." Tony knew that was bullshit. Maybe someday the sounds of battle, the gaping, wide-eyed faces of the dead, the wails of the wounded, will fade—become an old silent movie, then turn to dust and blow away. He prayed for this.

The three men sitting at the bar turned to see who walked in. The smiles and back pats followed.

"When did ya get back?" "How ya doin?" "Glad to see ya." "You're looking good." "How're the folks?"

He smiled back and tried to answer them.

Someone said, "get this guy a shot and a beer."

He sat on the stool that was offered to him and looked at the faces of the men around him.

There was Ernie, who survived the infantry. He was discharged early in the war because of wounds inflicted in Italy. Tony couldn't see the scars, but knew his body was riddled with them. He heard about how Ernie almost died.

There was Ben, who somehow survived Iwo Jima. Lost an eye there and got sent home. Tony knew the patch was a source of pride.

There was Stanley. Everyone called him Stashu. He survived dozens of battles. Was at Dachau when the gates were opened. Told everyone that was worse than any battle he had been in. He told everyone that he was haunted by the tortured victims, afraid that he was looking into the eyes of a relative left behind when his family immigrated to the United States.

There was Vick, the bartender. Too old to serve but was there when needed. He was there to serve the shots and beers to the nervous parents, wives, and girlfriends in the neighborhood. He was there to toast the dead and console the living. He listened to the stories that the families, wives, and girlfriends told when all they had now were memories and a tattered Western Union telegram.

"So you got a job?" Ben asked.

"Yeah. I got hired this morning at Crane's over on Kedzie," he replied. "My father wanted me to go back to work at the stockyards with him."

"Ya don't want to do it?" Stashu asked. "They pay good."

"Nah. Dirty work. Had enough of that." He didn't want to add that he'd seen enough blood and guts to last a lifetime. The smell of rotted cattle and horses on village farms haunted him like the other memories.

The men nodded.

"Besides, I'm thinking about going back to school. The GI bill, ya know, will pay for it. Maybe I can do something in a nice building instead of a factory."

"You're a smart kid," Vick added. "Go work at a bank or someplace like that."

"Yeah, that's what I'm thinking about."

They shared stories that were on the periphery. He knew by now that if you bragged about battles or killings you weren't there. The ones that were there couldn't bring themselves to talk about it. Shove it away and move on. Make it a part of the silence. Get a job. Raise a family. Live a good life.

There were so many that would never get the chance.

It was near the evening hour and more of the regulars were showing up.

Tony poked Ernie in the arm when he saw an old man take the stool at the end of the bar.

"Ain't that Father Bruno?" he asked.

"Yeah. Some priest he is," Ernie answered, making no attempt to hide his disgust. "Now he's the town drunk. He hits all the taverns, hoping someone will buy him a drink. The other priests sometimes show up and lug him back to the rectory."

"I remember when I was an altar boy," Tony told them. "We always had to empty the cruet to fill his chalice up. Then he'd guzzle it down like he was dying of thirst. It cracked us up."

"Yeah, well, it makes me sick," Ben interjected. "Through this whole stinkin' war, he didn't do shit for the people in his parish. Just got drunk. Could barely make it through a mass, much less a funeral or a wedding. They should just put him in a home somewhere. He's useless."

"Hey Father," yelled Stashu at the old man. "How's Jesus Christ doing? You talk to him lately."

The old priest nodded. "I talk to him all day, all day. He says to say bless you all. You good men. Me not so much."

"Ah, fer Cris sake, he's already loaded," Vick said.

He walked over to the priest.

"Listen, Padre," he told him. "Go back to the rectory. The people around here don't need to see this."

"Just one shot. I got money."

"Yeah, money that these hard-working people put in the basket on Sunday. So just leave, or I'll call the rectory and tell them to come and get you."

The priest looked back at the bartender, wiped his mouth with his handkerchief and nodded. He got off the stool and looked around. When he spotted Tony, he walked over to him.

"Tony, Tony. You back."

"Yeah, Father, I'm back.

"You okay?"

"Yeah, Father. I'm okay."

"You have a drink to celebrate."

"Yeah, I'm celebrating."

"You buy me a drink. I celebrate with you."

Tony looked down at the yellowed, bloodshot eyes and leathery skin of the old priest. He shook his head.

"No, Father. I ain't buying you a drink. Go back to the rectory. You should just get out of here. Vick's right. No one wants to see you like this. You're a priest. Act like one."

The priest gave him a small nod of defeat. He looked over at the others.

"Yes, okay, so I go now. I go," he said to the men. "You come to mass tomorrow, six o'clock mass. I see you there."

"Like hell you will," Ben tuned on his stool and faced the priest. "I'm never stepping my foot in a fucking church for the rest of my life. God died when the Japs bombed Pearl Harbor and Hitler rode into Poland. Got no use for any of that God bullshit."

"I know," Father Bruno said with an empty stare. "I know. It's bullshit. All bullshit."

With that he staggered away and out the door.

The four men exchanged glances and broke into laughter.

"Telling off a priest," Ernie said. "We're going to hell, for sure."

"Too late for that," Tony replied. "We've already been there."

Ben downed his shot and uttered to his friends. "That's for damn sure,"

A silence followed, the men suddenly unable to speak.

Tony broke through.

Wiping his mouth, he said, "I better get going. Any more shots like this and someone'll have to carry me home."

"Hey, whadya saying, Tone?" Stashu slurred. "It's Friday night. The girls will be here."

"The girls?"

"Yeah," Ben added. "After work. They've been working in the plants. Hell, my own sister worked on B-29 engines over at that Dodge City plant on Pulaski. Go figure. And she liked it."

"And my wife, Rita, worked over there with her," Ernie said. "Hell, someone had to do it. And they did a damn good job, too."

"My sisters are over at Western Electric," Tony told them. "So far, they still have jobs."

"Well, they can stop now. The GIs are back. You all need the jobs and they need to make the babies. Like before," Stashu said.

"Yeah, so," Vick interjected, laying yet another beer in front of Tony. "Every Friday and Saturday night, they show up. No matter what happens, they're here. Never thought I'd see the day when there were more dames than men in this place. The damn war. Everything is upside down."

"But," he added, "They're okay. Lotsa fun, most of the time. Don't get in fights like the old coots around here do."

"I wonder," Ernie said. "If that's gonna keep on happening, what with the boyfriends and husbands, most of them back now."

"Yeah, most of them," Vick repeated. "Lotsa tears shed in this place the last couple of years. More prayers here than in church."

"Did ya hear about Ann's guy Mike?" Ben asked his friends.

"Mike who?" Tony asked. "Ann who?"

"Ann V." Ernie said. "Drawing a blank. Forget the last name. There were seven of them over on Wolcott."

"Yeah, yeah, I know who you mean," Tony replied. "Went to school with a couple of them. What happened?"

"She was engaged to this guy, Mike McKay, a red-headed Irishman of all things," Ben said. "Not sure how he sneaked into this neighborhood? But anyway, he makes it through D-Day, even goes marching into Paris. Dies a few weeks before the war ends. Small town in Germany—some sniper from a window."

"I heard old Mike got the last word in," Stashu said. "He threw a grenade and hit his mark, even though he was shot and bleeding. Died later in the day."

"Ann's having a tough time," Vick said. "Hell, she was making her wedding dress when she found out. They planned on getting married as soon as they could after he got home. A dirty shame."

Tony said nothing. *Another horror story to add to the list.*

Minutes later, with a gust of wind, the door opened and in walked the girls with a blast of color and chatter and giggles.

Tony couldn't help but smile at the change they brought into the gloomy place. When he spotted his sister, he laughed. Everyone was soon caught up in the brightened mood. Everyone except Ann. She wasn't hard to miss.

Short and pretty, but with a look, an air. Something that Tony was so familiar with; not just sadness, but anger and despair. A look that could not be erased with forced laughter or false smiles.

The girls seemed to be everywhere and soon the jukebox was ringing out with swing music. The mood affected everyone in the tavern; everyone except Ann.

She sidled up next to Tony.

"Highball, please Vick."

"Sure thing, Ann." Vick said.

She looked over at Tony while she waited.

"I know you. Tony, right?"

"Yeah, I went to school with your brother, Leo."

"Yeah, Leo."

"How's he doing?"

"Leo, he's fine. Flat-footed bastard got out of the war. Sold shit on the black market. A real patriot. Kept me in nylons though."

Vick brought her drink.

"How you doing, Ann?" he asked, shaking his head no when she tried to pay.

"Trying to get through every day. That's all I can do. No words, Vick. No words can cover it."

He nodded. "I'm here, if ya do need to talk."

"I know Vick. Thanks"

She looked over at Tony and asked,

"Did you just get back?"

"Yeah, a couple of days ago."

She downed her drink and said nothing.

"I heard what happened. Really sorry," he said.

"Were you in Europe?"

He nodded.

"North Africa, Italy, France."

"You saw a lot of shit."

"Don't suppose by some miracle, you knew him. Mike, Mike McKay?"

"Nope, sorry. Wish I did. Sounds like he was a hell of a guy."

"He was. He was a hell of a guy. A great guy, and he was my guy."

Tears welled up. She wiped them away and motioned to Vick for a refill.

"So, you're home safe and sound. He's not. How the hell does that happen? Luck, destiny, what?"

"I ask myself that a dozen times a day. Don't know. Sometimes that question can make ya nuts, especially when you see what people like you are going through."

"I'm just so mad, so goddamned mad," she said. "Ya know. More than anything, I'm just plain pissed off. I look at you and I get mad. You survived. I should be glad for you. But you, someone I don't even know, and I get pissed off just looking at you."

"I understand. Believe me I do. Sometimes I feel guilty for not getting killed. How nuts is that?"

"Pretty nuts. Pretty damned crazy. You better make the best of it."

"Yeah, I'll try."

She slugged down the rest of her highball and motioned to Vick for another one.

"So now what do we talk about when there's no damned war to talk about," she said. "Seems like that's all we talked about forever."

He gave a slight laugh.

"Ya know, I'm not sure. I'm not even sure how to talk to someone who's not in the military. What do I say to people? What can I talk about with you that ain't gonna make you cry or give me the shakes?"

"You got a point. Music. Let's talk about music."

"Okay. Who's that playing on the jukebox?"

"Frank Sinatra. You know who he is, don't you?"

"Heard of him."

"Well let me tell you about this little runt, Frank Sinatra. After I get another drink."

"I need another one too and then you just tell me about this Frank Sinatra guy, and I'll tell you about Bob Hope and Glenn Miller."

After another round of drinks, the subject changed and so did the mood.

"I got a car," she said abruptly, interrupting his Bob Hope story.

"What?"

"Yeah, I got my father's car. I even have gas in it. Want to go for a drive? This place is too noisy and smoky."

"Yeah, yeah, sure. Let's go for a ride. I could use some fresh air. I've been here a while."

"Drive over to 43rd Street, by the old coal yard," Ann said after they got in the car. "It's after hours. The place is deserted."

Tony said nothing and drove on.

There was no pretention, no explanations, no words. They sank into each other arms, both attempting to smother an indescribable far-off throbbing ache.

"I ain't no tramp," Ann said, once their breathing slowed and the night air blew into the car. "Just because I did this, just because I wanted this, it don't make me a tramp."

"I know you're not a tramp," Tony replied. "I would never say that about you, never."

"Mike and I use to stop here. This old empty place, there's no one here to see you at night. It's ugly, but private, ya know."

"Yeah, I know."

He heard her gulp down a sob and said nothing.

"God, I miss him so much."

He held her tighter.

"I just needed to be held again. Does that make sense? By a man."

"Yeah, it makes sense. I need to feel like a human again. Not some creature who just kills and kills. When you're not killing or trying not to get killed, you're just scared. It ain't natural. I was afraid of what was happening to me. Does that make sense?"

"Un huh. I understand. I was getting like that. Everywhere you turned, someone was crying, someone you knew was dead or wounded. I got so I didn't care no more. How horrible is that?"

"It's not horrible. It's trying to survive. We did it on the battlefield, but you had to do it here, too."

"It was worse for you guys, for Mike."

"Yeah, that's not to say a lot of people here didn't go through hell too. Some worse than others."

"But when I heard about Mike, I can't explain it. It changed me. I know I'll never get over it, never. I loved him so much."

"Wish I had someone who loved me like that. He was a lucky man."

They wrapped each other in silence, consuming their own thoughts.

"I should take you home," Tony finally said.

"Yeah, maybe you should."

"I meant what I said, Ann. I can't describe it, but I needed this night. I needed a woman. I needed you."

"And I needed you too. Damn nuns and priests don't know what the hell they're talking about, saying this is a sin. It ain't. It takes you someplace and you come back and feel like a person again."

"Well said. Do you want me to call you in a few days?"

"Hell, no Tony. I don't need a boyfriend. I'm not ready for that."

"Glad you said that, cuz I don't need a girlfriend."

They both laughed.

After getting dressed, he drove to her house. They both got out of the car.

"I shoulda dropped you off first," she said.

"I don't mind the walk. I think I need it."

She took his hands.

"I'll never forget this night, Tony, never."

"I won't either, Ann. I know I won't."

"See ya around."

"Yeah," he said with a smile. "See ya around."

He never saw Ann again. He started taking classes at the University of Illinois at Navy Pier but kept on working. He rarely went to the tavern, partly because he didn't want to run into her, partly because he didn't want to see the men at the bar. Some memories had to be smothered, not shared. He kept busy.

It was a couple of months after the night with Ann that he stopped in at Vick's on a Saturday afternoon. The World Series would be blasting on Vick's radio. It seemed a good reason to go.

Vick looked pleased to see him.

"How ya doin, Tone? We hardly ever see ya around. What's going on?"

"Hard at work and hard at school."

"Heard from your folks that you're studying to be a teacher."

"Yeah, that's right. History and English. It's something I think I'll enjoy. Saw a lot of interesting things in Europe, when we weren't fighting—castles and churches. It was something. I want to go back some day and see it all in a different way. I have some good stories to share. It wasn't all bad. Kids need to hear that stuff."

"Right you are, Tony. Right you are," Vick said.

He brought him over a cold beer, before Tony asked for one.

"Did you hear about Ann?"

Tony froze.

"Ann?"

"Yeah, Ann. You two were pretty chummy a few weeks back. Don't tell me you don't remember her."

"I remember her. Of course, I do. What about her?"

"She got married today, this morning."

"What?"

"To Wally Wenkowski. Some old boyfriend. Word is she's knocked up. Got herself in a family way."

Tony froze.

"Makes you wonder if he's even the father. You know how people talk. Word is that he's nuts about her and is doing right by her. Someone else knocked her up."

Tony met Vick's gaze.

"Makes you wonder, don't it, Tony? Makes you wonder."

Tony looked down at his beer. He watched the bubbles floating up to the white foam.

He could feel Vick's eyes on him.

"You going to drink that or just stare at it?"

He stared at the beer a while longer.

Then turned and walked out the door…in silence.

PROM OF '68

Janet tried to ignore the stagnant, familiar odors of the Archer Avenue bus as it made its way downtown. She tried to block the sight of the shabby structures that housed businesses and families. It increased the misery that she was feeling.

It was prom day. The day she dreamed of since entering high school. The day she would walk down the front stairs of the three-flat where she lived. The day the neighbors would come out of their flats to see her. Her parents would take pictures. Her date would beam with pride.

Her dress, which she would have made, would bring oohs and aahs from everyone. A soft pale yellow with a white lace overlay, sleeveless with an empire waist, a yellow velvet ribbon covering the seam line. In anticipation of this day, she bought the pattern and fabric from Marshall Field's at the beginning of Senior year.

How naïve and stupid I am, she thought bitterly as the bus jerked to another stop. *What is wrong with me? I'm such an idiot. Why would anyone want to take me to the prom? Me, with dishwater hair that couldn't hold a curl, sad-sack hazel eyes, skinny and small-chested. I should have known better. All I had to do was to look in the mirror. What guy would want to be seen in public with me?*

When April came and went and Janet still had no boyfriend, much less a date for the prom, resignation set in. When her well intentioned mother suggested that she go with her cousin, she fled from the house in tears.

The time needed to make the dress, also came and went. The prom, now a painful subject to Janet, was the topic of conversation in all her classes.

Initially she blamed her dateless situation on the fact that she went to an all-girl Catholic high school, but the other girls had dates, and some had steady boyfriends. Two girls said they were engaged—something the nuns couldn't find out about.

Even the boys that she worked with at the department store either showed no interest or had girlfriends.

As the date neared she tearfully packed the fabric, the lace, the ribbon, and the pattern away hoping that someday, the lace might be a part of her wedding dress. But even that thought seemed like another fanciful daydream.

The bus rambled on and Janet fought back tears. Going downtown was her form of consolation. She loved downtown Chicago. And she loved Marshall Field's the most. To her it was the hub of fashion and class. Then there was Carson's, the next best. She could spend hours browsing those stores and the other department stores that lined State Street. It would have to be browsing only; most items were unaffordable. From there she would walk through the Palmer House just to admire the artistry of the lobby. She never sat down or walked too slowly. She knew that she didn't belong there, and a hotel employee would surely throw her out if she lingered. But she loved that beautiful, ornate structure and fantasized that she would stay there someday with her husband.

The bus finally came to a stop on State and Madison. When she got off, she couldn't help but note that the weather was perfect for a prom—a beautiful, sunny May day. Another reason to be miserable.

As she walked through aisles in Marshall Field's, she knew it was a bad idea. She became more depressed. She decided to go to the Art Institute instead, then Grant Park and Buckingham Fountain, but was hit with pangs of hunger. It occurred to her that she hadn't eaten since breakfast. She decided to get something to eat before heading over to the museum. She decided on the little restaurant near the Museum with its photos of celebrities that covered the walls. The food was good, the place was casual, and she never felt self-conscious eating there alone. She headed in that direction.

Greg looked down at the smiling little Chinese man. A dollar. The man was giving Greg a one-dollar tip. One dollar for a table of eight—eight Chinese tourists who could barely understand the menu, which forced Greg to explain what each dish was. One dollar for two hours of taking dishes back and forth to the kitchen because they still didn't understand what they were getting. One dollar for his forced, tight-lipped smile, while the other servers were making a lot more than a dollar during the busy lunch hour.

Greg didn't return the smile as they shook his hand and left the restaurant. He wanted to follow them. He hated this job. The long hours, the hard-to-please customers, the miserable boss, and most of all, the lousy tips.

Now here came Alphonse, ambling through the door. The customer every server hated. Alphonse, overweight by at least a hundred pounds, always sweaty, with small eyes that seemed buried in his face. Alphonse, with the condescending attitude and ridiculous demands. A friend to Stavros, the owner, a fact that made him feel that insulting the food and the servers was his right.

He was going over to one of Greg's tables. With a smirk and a nod, he gestured to Greg. Greg bit his lip as he walked to the table. Alphonse began with the usual insult directed at the cook in the kitchen, saying that it was beyond his capabilities to make a proper Monte Carlo sandwich, so he was being forced to order soup and a salad.

"The lettuce better be crispy and there should be no sign of radishes in it. And I want the tomatoes cut into one-inch pieces." he told Greg.

Greg nodded and started to walk away.

"You do understand what I just said. Because you don't look too bright."

Greg turned and looked into Alphonse's beady little eyes.

"What did you just say?"

"I said you don't look too bright. A fair assessment. Otherwise why would you be doing this servile job?"

And that was Greg's breaking point.

"You know what, Alphonse? Fuck you!" he screamed, loud enough for most of the customers to hear. "Get your own goddamn food, you miserable, fat, condescending pig."

Alphonse sputtered a response, but Greg was on his way out.

Stavros watched the exchange and before he had a chance to act, Greg shoved his pen and pad in Starvros's chest.

"You can wait on your disgusting friend, because I'm done. I quit. I've had enough of your bullshit and all the bullshit that comes with this place."

He stomped out the door, leaving an opened-mouthed Stavros in his wake.

Janet was two tables away from Alphonse. She heard the exchange. Once Greg walked out, she began to laugh and laugh loudly. Other customers joined in, to Alphonse's embarrassment. She left a good tip for her server, paid her bill, and left the restaurant.

Janet spotted Greg at the corner opposite the Art Institute. Even though the light had changed, he didn't cross the street. He was pacing.

She approached him.

"It was a good thing, what you did in there," she said to him.

"Oh, crap, you saw that," he said.

"I was two tables over. And you were right. He's a fat, condescending pig."

"I am so embarrassed. I'm sorry you had to hear that."

"I've heard worse."

"It was a bad day. I didn't need that jerk, but I did need the job."

Janet looked at the young man. He seemed close to her in age. He wasn't very tall but was very thin. Dark eyes with curled dark hair, long but not long enough to consider him a hippie.

"I'm Janet, by the way. I don't normally approach guys I don't know, but I was glad you did what you did. I can't stand nasty people. If it were me, I probably would have just taken it and cried later. I just wanted you to know."

"Thanks. It did kinda feel good," he said with a grin. "I'm Greg."

"Hi, Greg."

"Hi, Janet," he said. "You a tourist?"

"No, I live in Chicago. Just spending the day downtown."

"I'm heading over to Grant Park. Want to join me? It's peaceful there. I like to sit and stare at the fountain for a while. It always makes me feel better. You know."

"Yeah. I like it there, too," she said, forgetting about her plans for the Art Institute. "It's one of my favorite places."

"So, you want to go?"

"Yeah, sure, okay," Janet replied while saying a silent prayer that this wasn't the dumbest thing she had done in a while.

They slowly worked their way through the usual crowd that converged on Michigan Avenue without talking.

When they got to the fountain, they stood in silence as they took in the sight before them.

The beauty and the power of the fountain remained unchanged, every summer of every year.

"Every time I stand before this fountain and feel the spray of water it always feels like it's the first time I'm seeing it," she said. "It's hard not to be in awe. You know what I mean?"

Greg looked over at her.

"Yeah, I know what you mean. I guess I feel the same way. That's why I always end up coming here."

He added, "It looks ancient, doesn't it? But it's only been here since 1927."

"I know. A rich lady had it built in honor of her brother," she replied.

"Most people don't know a thing about it. They just come here to take pictures. To me it's a work of art."

Janet looked over at him and smiled. He returned the smile.

They turned away and walked toward Grant Park.

Without the tumult of the fountain's water, they found it easier to talk.

"So, Janet," Greg began. "Where in Chicago do you live?"

Janet felt a pang of embarrassment, which she usually did when someone outside of her neighborhood asked that question. She wanted to lie but didn't.

"Southside. Back of the Yards."

"The stockyards?" He sounded shocked.

She cringed.

"Well, I don't live *in* the stockyards. I'm a few miles away."

"That so. I never met anyone from there. What's it like?

"It smells bad sometimes," she said. "Depending on the wind. Houses are crummy. Mostly two flats and a lot of taverns. All the old people are from the old country, wherever that is? Maybe Poland or Lithuania, wherever. A lot of churches. Nuns and priests are always in your business, just like the old ladies."

"You sure paint a pretty picture of the place."

"I know," she said, surprised at her own anger that shrouded the place where she was raised.

"I can't wait until I'm out of school and get a full-time job. Then I'm moving out. My parents don't know that yet. They're in no hurry to leave. My father probably can't stand the thought of living on a block that doesn't have a tavern on it. My mother was literally born in that house. She said she's not going anywhere. A lot of people are leaving though. So I'll leave too and without my parents."

When he didn't respond, Janet looked away in embarrassment. Saying goodbye and walking away now seemed like a good idea.

"I'm from Rogers Park," he blurted out.

"Where's that? In the suburbs?"

"No," he said with a short laugh. "It's a neighborhood on the North Side of the city."

"Oh. Well I don't know too much about the rest of this city. When you're a Southsider, that's all you know. The White Sox and Bridgeport. I didn't even know about the Cubs for a long time. I just figured that the Sox were the only team in Chicago."

Greg laughed out loud.

Janet knew she was turning a very dark shade of red.

"That's funny," he said.

"No, it's not. I better go before I make a complete ass out of myself."

"No. Don't go. I'm sorry if I embarrassed you. I don't think you're stupid or anything, just uninformed, I guess."

"Some of them can't even figure out why I spend so much time downtown. I should love it there. Get married to another Lithuanian, have kids and go to the Lithuanian church, blah blah. Just like they all did. They don't know that if I stay there, I'll go crazy."

She added, "So tell me about Rogers Park," after an abrupt silence.

"It's okay. We're by the lake. Far north side. Evanston is real close. My parents have an apartment in this old high-rise on the twelfth floor. It's them and my sister and me."

"Sounds nice."

"It is, I guess. Nothing fancy. I like living by the lake."

"What do your parents do?"

"My dad works at Continental Bank. My mom used to teach but stopped when we came along. Says it's a different world now and doesn't want to teach again. So she volunteers a lot, usually with some Jewish organization."

"Jewish?"

"Yeah, I'm a Jew."

"You are?"

"Yeah. Does that bother you?"

"No. It's just that I never met a Jewish person before, except for the peddler that used to come around once in a while and the guy at the hardware store."

"You really do have a lot to learn."

"Yeah, I know."

"Well I never met a Lithuanian from the Back of the Yards before. So we're even."

"I guess we are."

"Are you still in high school?" he asked.

"Yeah, graduating next month, from the all-girl Catholic high school. Can't wait for that day to come either. What about you?"

"Graduated last year. Just finishing up my first year at Circle."

"Circle?"

"The University of Illinois at Circle Campus. Everyone calls it Circle."

"Oh. Once again, I'm showing how little I know. What are you studying?"

"The basics now. My father wants me to get a degree in business. I'm not sure if that's what I want. I'm looking into Criminal Justice. Maybe I'll go into law or law enforcement," he answered. "What about you? You're going to need a good job, before you can get an apartment."

"I did take business classes—steno, typing, that stuff, but the thought of being a secretary doesn't do it for me. It sounds so boring. I work part-time at the neighborhood department store now. I'd like to work at Marshall Field's if they'd have me. I love fashion. I make a lot of my own clothes. I'd really like to be a designer of women's clothes. Don't even know how to go about that though. I don't have the money for college; either do my parents. I guess I'll just have to see what happens."

"The same goes for me," he replied. "So what brings you to downtown Chicago on a Friday afternoon? Goofing off? Skipping out on the nuns?"

She hesitated, afraid the reason would make her look ridiculous.

"Yeah, I faked a real serious headache," she said. "They let me leave. Too nice of a day to sit there listening to a lot of stuff that I'm not interested in."

"A real rebel. Hope they don't find out the truth."

"At this point I really don't care. I just want out of that place."

Janet stood up and looked down at Michigan Avenue.

"I never get tired of looking at this city," she said. "Just look at those beautiful buildings. I love it down here. I do hope I can get hired at Field's or even Carson's."

Greg joined her.

"Yeah, I think sometimes I get so used to seeing it all I don't really appreciate it how nice it is."

They began walking with no destination in mind.

"My brother just got drafted," she told him. "We're all worried that he might get sent to Vietnam. I really don't understand this war. It scares me."

The conversation then veered to recent history; the assassination of Martin Luther King, the riots that made Janet fear the city was burning down when she saw flames from her bedroom window. They shared their stories.

"This is some pretty heavy talk," Greg said. "I'd rather talk about music."

"Yeah, me too. Okay. I love the Beatles, the Stones and Crosby, Stills and Nash."

"Yeah. Me too, but you got to love The Who and Jimmy Hendrix."

They eventually ended up strolling on Michigan Avenue, with no pause in their conversations.

"I really like Donavan, especially…." Janet's voice trailed off. She stopped walking.

She looked around and realized that they were standing in front of the Conrad Hilton Hotel. A limousine had pulled up and several couples were getting out. Young couples, well-off young couples, obviously going to their prom. The young men in tuxedos, the girls in the most stylish of gowns.

"What?" Greg said, annoyed that the sudden appearance of these couples blocked their way.

Janet didn't speak, but watched the couples go past, the doormen greeting them as they entered the grand hotel. Several of them looked over at Janet and Greg.

"What," he repeated when he saw her fascination with the group. "It's just a bunch of rich kids going to their prom."

"I didn't tell you the truth when you asked me why I was downtown today."

"Okay. Not that it matters. Not really any of my business."

"Today is my prom. I'm down here because I had no one to go with me. No boyfriend, no kind of date at all. So I came down here instead. Alone, of course."

"Oh, okay," he muttered.

"I know it sounds stupid, but it was something I couldn't wait for from the first day of high school. But, no date, no prom. Kinda depressing."

"It doesn't sound stupid."

"It sounds pathetic. I couldn't even dig up one date for the prom. It was awful having to tell the girls in my class who were all excited about it, that I wasn't going. It was humiliating."

"I guess it would be for a girl. Not that big of a deal for a guy."

"Did you go to your prom?" she asked.

"Yeah. Did the whole thing with the corsage and pictures. It was okay, but I couldn't wait until it was over. Then it was fun. Ended up at a park by the lake. We all got drunk and did a lot of necking."

"You have a girlfriend?" she asked, now afraid of the answer.

"No. After graduation she left for college in California. Never heard from her again, although we both promised that we would write to each other. Never did. Strangely, it never bothered me. We just went our separate ways. That's what life is about, isn't it? Going your own way. Not stopping each other."

"Yeah, I guess."

They began walking again, their conversation now at a standstill.

Wide-eyed, Janet asked, "God, what time is it?"

"Quarter after six."

"I better go catch my bus. My parents will be frantic if I'm not home before dark. It's after rush hour and the buses will take forever."

"I'll walk you to your bus stop."

"Okay," she said with a smile.

"What about you?" she asked as they neared State Street.

"I'm in no hurry to go home. My parents will have a fit when they find out I walked out on my job. My sister will probably think it's funny. She has a strange sense of humor. It's not like we're rich or anything. People think because my dad works at a bank and since we're Jewish, we should have a lot of money. We don't."

Janet let him talk.

"College is expensive. If it wasn't, I wouldn't be going to Circle. I'd be at a real university somewhere."

"It's better than nothing," Janet replied. "And it can keep you out of Vietnam."

"That's not why I'm going."

She could see that she angered him.

"I didn't say that it was."

"Like I said, I'll probably end up in law enforcement."

"Okay."

State Street looked strangely deserted now that rush hour was over and most of the stores were closed.

"This is my favorite time down here. Even better when it's really late and dark," Greg said.

"Not scary."

"No. It's like a photograph. And it can be really quiet. One of the benefits of working in a restaurant on Michigan. I linger down here a lot. Maybe catch a late movie. When I come out, I just hang around and take it in. Love it."

"Sounds cool. I think I'd like to do that some time."

"You don't think it's weird?"

"No, kind of artsy. Not weird. Definitely not weird."

"In a little while," he continued, "the lines will start at the theatres, especially at The Chicago and the Oriental. Then the restaurants start to fill up."

She looked around, trying to see it through his eyes.

"State Street, that great street," he said. "Makes me glad I live here."

Janet stopped walking and pointed up.

"My stop. The old Archer Avenue bus."

"How long will it take to get home?"

"Not too long. Depends on how long I have to wait for the bus on Ashland," she said. "What about you?"

"I catch the El. Then walk part of the way. Not bad."

Janet looked down the street to see if the bus was near. It was.

"Janet."

"Yes."

"Is it okay if I call you? Maybe we can catch a movie or something. Go for another walk."

"I'd like that, Greg. I'd like that a lot."

She fumbled around in her purse for a pen and paper.

"All I have is the receipt from the restaurant where I had an unforgettable lunch."

They both laughed as she wrote her number on the piece of paper, the bus now on the next block.

"Good," Greg said, looking down at the piece of paper. "I'll call you."

"Okay. Good. Great," she replied lightly.

"Janet,"

"Yes,"

"I would have taken you to the prom."

"I would have been happy to go with you, Greg."

The bus was squealing to a stop a few feet away.

"Janet,"

"Yes."

He reached over and took her hand and squeezed it.

"I'll see you soon."

A shiver ran through her.

She nodded; words suddenly trapped in her throat.

She almost tripped as she forced herself to get through the open bus door.

Sitting in a seat by the window, she turned and watched him until he was no longer in view.

There was no attempt to hide the smile on her face.

Janet was very glad she didn't go to the prom.

ABOUT THE AUTHOR

SANDRA COLBERT is originally from Chicago. She is the author of *Chicago Bound*, which is a collection of short stories about the Back of the Yards area in Chicago. She is also the author of the Kate Harrison detective series. She is on the Board of The Chicago Writers Association as well as a member of The Society of Midland Authors. Sandra currently lives in Rockford with her husband and pets.